Change State

Adventures in the Liaden Universe® Number 32

Sharon Lee and Steve Miller

Thanks

Our thanks to Lauretta Nagel, for vetting the sciency bits

And

To the Mighty Tyop Hunters

Bruce Glassford, Eric Shivak, Linda Shoun, Jim Smith

for their eagle eyes

Any typos or infelicities that remain in the text

are the fault of the authors

Copyright Page

Change State

Adventures in the Liaden Universe® Number 32

Pinbeam Books: pinbeambooks.com

#

#

"Dead Men Dream" is original to this chapbook.

"Command Decision," was previously published in *Release the Virgins*, Michael A. Ventrella, editor, Fantastic Books, 2018.

#

Cover design by: selfpubbookcovers.com/Visions

ISBN: 978-1-948465-16-8

Author's Foreword

You may have heard about that PO Box in Sandusky, Ohio. Or maybe the one in Poughkeepsie, NY, both claimed as a prime source by professional writers in answer to the perennial question, "Where do you get your story ideas?"

In fact, story ideas are just that hard, or that easy, to get, and they come from lots of sources, not all involving a secretive special address rousted from the back-ads of *Writer's Digest* or *The New Yorker*. In fact today there's an easier way: just watch for what anthology editors want and then listen to your brain to see if you can hear an echo that might just be what the editor needs.

The two stories in this chapbook were both born of that last approach. In the case of "Command Decision," an anthology editor familiar with our work came to us (that would be to Steve Miller and Sharon Lee together) and said approximately, "I like what you do—can you do your take on a story that uses the phrase *release the virgins* as a turning point or fulcrum in the story?"

Wow, could we! Sharon and I both had ideas—and after a short confusion, we both wrote separate stories for that anthology under our own names.

There were, you understand, seventeen stories written for that anthology and each of them very different from the others. Sharon's story, "The Vestals of Midnight," is set in her Archers Beach universe and is NOT included in this chapbook. My story, "Command Decision," is set in the Liaden Universe®, and is offered here as a reprint.

The second story, "Dead Men Dream," was destined at first for an anthology about derelicts, an anthology that will soon be published without "Dead Men Dream." That editor was looking for stories of under six thousand words, adhering tightly to theme. Sharon and I started out thinking we might be able to fit a derelict-coming-to-life story into the basic theme and length.

We discovered as we worked that our characters in "Dead Men Dream," who'd been briefly introduced in *Trade Secret*, our 2013 Liaden Universe® novel, had more to learn, more to say, and more to dream, than we expected. While effectively inspired by the anthology theme, the ideas for this were larger than we'd known and rather than remove three words out of four we elected to keep what we had. We wrote another story for the anthology, *Derelict:* "Standing Orders."

In the meantime, "Dead Men Dream" comes to you as an original story, published in for the first time in this chapbook.

Enjoy!

Steve Miller

Waterville Maine

February 2021

Dead Men Dream

Sharon Lee and Steve Miller

ONE

Even dead men have to eat.

It fell to Khana to forage for two such, and he was pleased to do so, for the necessity put him out among people, allowed him opportunity for exercise, and to improve his language.

This morning's foraging was nearly done. He had eaten his breakfast, and had the second in-hand, needing only to show the ID to the lad behind the counter and be on his way. However, he had another mission, aside food, and he asked about Malvern's continued absence.

A smile was his first answer, and Khana was once more surprised to find that this open betrayal of emotion was a. . .comfort.

"Don't you worry," the boy—Miki, according to the badge on his shirt—said cheerfully, "she'll be back after she finishes her tour. She's a Reservist, and they call her up now and then."

Khana moved his head slowly side to side—this was a new gesture for him, and he feared that this was one of the times when he had failed of accurately displaying nuance, for the boy reached out and patted his arm, as one offering comfort.

"Oh no, it's not a sad thing! She did the work for twenty years and plus, but even once you're done, you're not *really* done, if you know what I mean?"

The boy was—yes, a boy; surely younger than Bar Jan, though much larger. He was Terran of the type the InfoBooklet claimed as "Port Chavvy Born, " his hair dark and long, and dark hair also on the lower part of his pale face.

"I mean," Khana said slowly in his careful new-learned Terran, "that I do *not* know what you mean. As you know—" here he waved his *ticket* that was at once ID, room key, permission to eat on *Chavvy's cred*, and entree to those places he was permitted to go on station, including this kitchen, "I am not from around here, myself."

"Oh, oh, right, I forgot! Sorry! You're a reg'lar and always glad to see you, and I just—well. Been here my whole life, is what. I forget things is different elseplace. Some day, maybe, I'll land on a planet!"

There came a chime from a piece of equipment behind him.

"Be a sec," he said, turning to open a small baking unit, and using the paddle to slide out a pan of cheese muffins.

"There, let those cool a bit," he said, coming back to the counter, and bestowing another smile on Khana.

"See, when you're born here, or if you take the course and go for Port Resident—gotta swear to do that—but it's the same thing, really, 'cause that means you're took care of if you die here, and Port Chavvy admits you live here if you go offstation and get in trouble Out There." He snapped his fingers, a gesture to which Khana could attach no ready meaning.

"I remember! It's called *citizen,* Out There. So being a *citizen* of the Port means you got responsibilities, and you gotta do service for three years wherever the Port needs you. After you're done your three years, though, you're on Reserve—a Reservist. That means you get called up in every little while, so somebody else can have a break, or to keep what you know fresh. So here's Chief Malvern, she served for seven turns—she wears those little pins, you might've seen 'em. Officially, she can't be made to serve again full-time, so now they just call her up whenever they need her. An' that's where she is now—called up to fix something. I mean, Malvern knows it all—*done all the spots*, is what we say—and knows Port Chavvy inside out."

"I see," Khana said, bowing slightly in thanks. It was not done on Port Chavvy, the nuanced bow, there was none to read them, after all. However, it was allowed, the small inclination, as a thanks.

"Is it permitted to ask the nature of your own service?"

Miki's pale face reddened, but there, he was a comely lad for all his size and it went well on him.

"Oh, well—I mean—me, I'm training on the fuel supply systems and such, but part-time dock help for the A deck, that's my official service spot. We don't have all that many big ones come in, I mean the last was that Liaden. . .oh."

Miki stopped, took a breath, glanced over his shoulder at the pan of cooling muffins, and looked back to Khana, cheeks still becomingly pink.

"So *eny-how*, yeah, we're trying to work out a service option that'll let me combine the fuel system stuff with the A Deck stuff. But, see, Chief Malvern, she has so much time in grade. . .you know what that means?"

Khana thought of Malvern, her modest uniform impeccably presented, always alert. She had the bearing of a commander, even if it was only a commander of pastry and hot food. That she had been a leader, he did not doubt.

"I think," Khana said, careful of his pronunciation, "that this is related to the concept I was taught as *melant'i*."

"Might be, might be," Miki allowed, "but yeah, so she gets the call 'cause even though she's not in the chain of command these days, she's the one who knows it all—all the systems, I mean, and how they work together, and—"

"Hey, Miki!" came a voice from behind. Startled, Khana turned to see a woman in a Port Chavvy volunteer duty vest waving an ID card. She gave him a nod, which was mannerly, here. Khana returned it.

"Them cheese muffins ready to be 'preciated?"

"Sure are!" the boy snatched a carry box, and turned to the tray he had put to cool. "How many?"

"Just the one today, they got me workin' solo, inventoryin' the aid closets. I'll be grabbing a cup of caf on the way out, too."

"You got it." Miki handed the box over, the worker slid the card through the reader, and that quick was gone, stopping briefly at the entrance to draw a cup of the hot, bitter drink that on Port Chavvy served as "work tea."

Khana turned back to the counter, thinking that he had taken up enough of the lad's time, but Miki wasn't done yet.

"So yeah, Malvern, she knows Port Chavvy inside out, like they say. An' she was right here behind this counter, doin' the dinner prep, setting the breads up to rise and all, when her comm buzzes. She listens for maybe two minutes, puts it away in her pocket and says to Baydee, 'I been attached for a few days, Hon. Keep the griddles in tune for me, right? And call upstairs to ask himself to tend to my breads.'"

"So yeah, it was sudden." Miki frowned, and leaned forward a little. "If this is rude, you just tell me so, all right, and no offense to me, nor meant to you, but I wonder—your friend. Ain't seen him for a while again. He doin' right fine? No troubles? Malvern worried, him bein' so broke up like he was."

This, Khana reminded himself, was not the seeking of advantage that it most certainly would have been in the society he had moved in before his summary death. No, this was kindness, very nearly kin-care, and was properly answered as such.

So.

"My. . .friend," Khana said carefully. "He grows stronger, though there is still pain. He was made sad when we last came here together, to find that Malvern was absent." He hesitated, wondering if he had said enough to satisfy—and it appeared that he had.

Miki nodded. "Yeah, everybody misses her. You tell 'im—your friend—that we miss him, too, and we're lookin' to see him again, when he's ready. An' you know what? I noticed he favors that dark loaf that none of us can get quite the way Malvern gets it? You tell your friend there's only one other baker on all Port Chavvy has Malvern's touch with that loaf. He's a top chef, an' it's hard to get him down here, but he'll be comin' to give us a hand alt-shift, and we'll be havin' the dark on hand, startin' tomorrow." He paused, and added. "Me 'n Baydee are gonna be standin' by as helpers, so might be we'll catch the way of it, this time."

That they had noticed so much, Khana told himself severely, was not dangerous. It was kindness, again, and he schooled himself to receive it as it was given.

"Thank you," he said. "I will tell him." He stopped short of saying that his friend would be pleased, and was saved from trying to introduce another question by a noisy bustle at the entrance to the Cantina.

Khana turned his head, espying a full work crew of ten, and looked back to Miki.

"Yeah, looks like I'm on," the lad said with a grin. "You take care now."

He turned down counter, raising a hand and calling out a greeting to "Reeves."

Khana took his carry box, and went out into the corridor.

#

It had become Khana's habit to take the long way home. Even on those infrequent occasions when Bar Jan accompanied him, they took the back hallways, his companion pronouncing them *interesting* with such sincerity that it had taken Khana two trips to realize that the most interesting thing about them was the scarcity of other travelers.

The benefit that Khana took from walking the back hallways arose from the fact that the route between Cantina and wayroom encompassed very nearly eight thousand of his short steps. The literature provided by the Port had suggested that the planet-born achieve ten thousand steps a day in order to retain a modicum of physical fitness while on station. Given the circumstances of their residence on Port Chavvy, it was unlikely that Khana would ever walk on a planet again. However, he dreamed—of flowers, and of Liad's green-blue day-sky, the taste of fresh air. He had visited the E Deck Atrium, once, and there had been flowers, trees, grass. At the time, he had been distressed by the lack of a sky, and the taste, still, of station air. Lately, he had been thinking that he might visit the atrium again.

Though not today.

There was an unusual amount of traffic in the back halls today, groups of people wearing gray overalls with the Port Chavvy logo on them. Some were inspecting doors and locks, others were occupied with the various cabinets and closets. He passed one worker who was staring into a closet lavishly decorated with the outlines of what must, Khana thought, be tools, masks, flasks. While some of the silhouettes were filled by the objects they represented, most—were not. The worker shook her head, and pulled a note-taker out of her pocket as he went by.

"Good thing we ain't *had* an emergency, s'all I can say," he heard her mutter.

At the intersection of hallways where his necessity took him to the right, there was a cluster of workers around several open closets, note-takers in some hands while others stood at ease, talking. Khana paused, looking for the best route through the crowd. One man looked up, saw him, and waved cheerfully.

"You come on ahead!" he called, and to his comrades, "Hey, make some room, why not? Commerce has gotta go forth!"

This was apparently a pleasantry, for those of the group laughed, or grinned, all in good humor, and arranged themselves so that Khana had a clear path through.

"Thank you," he said, loud enough, he hoped, to be heard by all.

"No problem," returned the man who had first noticed him. "We ain't paid to block the halls."

One of the inconveniences of traveling the back corridors was the lack of public newsfeeds. There was only one on the route between the wayrooms and the Cantina. Despite that, there were rarely more than three or four people paused to read the news, so Khana could be assured of finding a place where the screen was not blocked by tall Terrans.

Today, he was the only one attending the news at this hour. He put his box on the floor at his feet and looked up at the screen.

Most often, the news had nothing to do with him, but it gave him practice reading Terran, and also gave him something of real life to take to Bar Jan on those frequent days when he did not venture beyond the wayroom.

The background news-view today was of starry space, courtesy of the top-class restaurant he'd never been to up in the high decks. He glimpsed, *Oncoming trouble?* as a brief headline, but the colors changed then, and he saw he was fortunate to have arrived just as the scroll was finishing. There came a space of blank screen, followed by the Port Chavvy logo, and the scroll began again, from the top.

First was General Port News: there were corridor closures in the business section, a part of the station Khana had never seen. The five year inspection and repair of the water delivery system to the Administrative Level was scheduled for tonight alt-shift; offices were to be closed during the work.

Next came an announcement from Port Administration, and this—so seldom did the news impact his life that Khana read the announcement, and the next item was scrolling up before he realized that something—*advantageous*—was about to happen.

The next item summarized the findings of the recent audit of the station's shielding; the next, a list of Amended Departures; and, last, the daily update on the comet.

Khana scanned them all impatiently, waiting for the scroll to repeat, so he could read that interesting item again, to be certain that he had read correctly, and that—there!

Allotment Increases for Awaiting Rescue, Transport, or Skillful Habitation: Eight percent base rate; four percent volunteer rate; one percent facilitator rate. Medical stipend increase six percent. All increases effective next pay-in.

Khana's breath caught. He drew at base rate. Bar Jan received the medical stipend through his next appointment at the clinic. If he was declared "fit" then he also would draw at base rate.

Once Bar Jan was "fit," Khana would be free to apply himself to the volunteer listings, something that had been beyond his reach, and that rate has also increased. Combining those resources, they might move into larger quarters in the ARTS hallways where their current wayroom was located. The potential to improve their situation was unexpectedly exciting.

Khana's gaze had still been on the screen, though he had seen nothing but his own excited thoughts until the word UPDATE in bright red letters caught his attention.

The same image he'd seen before courtesy of the Long View restaurant appeared.

The trajectory of the inbound comet has changed. Attempts are being made to push it further from Port Chavvy. There is no danger to the station; the adjustments are being made merely to increase the distance between the comet and the station during its passage.

Khana stared at the screen as the image magnification picked up. Comets, asteroids, meteors—he'd not had much to do with space objects while caring for his master's needs, and before that, as a youth training to care for his master, he'd had only Liad's quiet skies overhead and his delm's admonition to always watch the skies, that the weather never show Rinork's heir to disadvantage.

Khana shook himself from the hypnotic image and the news scrolls. If all was well, all was well, and Bar Jan was waiting for his breakfast and his news.

* * *

Shanna was late returning with the meal.

In the downtime between the fifth and sixth *sets* of exercise, he weighed whether Shanna was late *enough* that he must begin to fear himself abandoned.

Again.

Not that there was any fault to find, if Shanna had decided to leave. The only question that might be asked was why he had waited so long. Well. There was also the question of why he had remained at all.

Surely, it would have been the better plan to have departed when Delm Rinork had declared Shanna's master dead, and ordered the body stripped of everything of value. Rinork by contract was bound to return servants of the clan to Liad, should their service end while off-world. Not even Rinork could lay blame on *Shanna*. She had been displeased with him, but Shanna knew the way around her anger. If he had exerted himself, abased himself, only a little—Rinork would have honored the contract, and taken Shanna home to Liad, where his own delm would most assuredly have been angry, though not so angry that Shanna need fear for his life.

The timer declared his rest interval done. He stood once more, made sure of the weights on his wrists, and began the next set.

Six sets of six was the rule, three times a day, until he felt that had become too easy. Tomorrow, he would promote himself to seven sets of seven. His goal was to achieve ten sets of ten by the time he was to return to the clinic for his next evaluation.

It was, by any accounting, a modest enough goal.

If Shanna were gone, he would need to do better.

Fear interrupted the working of the weights.

If Shanna were gone, he, himself, had no ID—Shanna had needed both in order to collect two meals. He, who had stayed in the room they shared, had nothing to prove his status with regard to the station, which fed him, and clothed him, and provided his medical care.

Swallowing, he forced himself to take up the interrupted rhythm of the weight work. There was no advantage to Shanna in keeping his ID, he told himself. The assertion did little to soothe him. Perhaps if he had known less about unscrupulous means, and the justifications for using them...

He worked through the prescribed routine, counting meticulously. When he had done, he sat down and removed the weights. Then he closed his eyes.

Shanna's absence, he told himself, had been longer than average, but not worrisomely so. He was hungry, that was what fretted him. Hunger made him impatient.

As did so many other things.

He opened his eyes and he brought his hands up for inspection. One was well-shaped and seemly, the fingers long and straight, the skin gold-toned and supple. The other—was a nightmare, wizened, with blotched pink skin. The reconstructed fingers were long and straight, but the merest pegs, all but strengthless muscles not yet fully reconstituted.

Which reminded him that he had yet to work with the pressure ball. Usually, he did his first session after breakfast was eaten. Today, with breakfast late—no.

No, he corrected himself. The book; recall the book—*change is opportunity*, so the book had it, a curiously Liaden sentiment, given a special poignancy by circumstances.

He rose and crossed the small room, opened the drawer where he kept the pressure ball when it was not in use, and took it up in his ruined—no, he caught himself up once more. Not ruined. Rebuilt. His hand had been rebuilt, even now it was useful for some small tasks. It would become more so, did he continue with his exercises.

So. Today, he had been given the opportunity to have an extra session with the pressure ball, thus speeding his healing.

There, that was positive. The book also taught the importance of a positive viewpoint. See the *benefit* of the situation, then work to improve it, that was the book's advice. This placed one in a position of strength and allowed a survey of circumstance through eyes untainted by anger or fear.

He worked the ball, and turned to consider the place in which he found himself.

It was a small room—which was, he reminded himself, good, for there was less for Shanna to maintain. The space was orderly, neat, and clean, for Shanna would never tolerate a room that was at sixes and twelves. Everything must be where he could immediately lay hand on it, to best to serve his master.

So, a small room, two beds that folded into the walls during waking hours; a table and two chairs; an upholstered chair; the set of drawers. An alcove next to the table held a cool-box, a tap into the station's water supply, and a single heating coil so that they might make tea, or warm leftover food without having to go out into the common area.

Next to the drawers was a discreet door which opened onto a basic accommodation, with a sonic shower.

How had he, once the named heir to the delm of Clan Rinork, come to occupy this tidy, tiny space, and stand grateful for it?

Ah, but that had to do with his—*error*.

In the realm of errors, his had been—spectacular. There, that followed the book's advice.

He had goaded a trader—a lad scarcely past halfling, his junior by several Standards, adopted son to one of the most well-connected and canny of the masters of trade—he had pursued and goaded this young trader into a duel.

Had all gone his way, he would have killed the young trader, the dueling set he had proposed to use having been tuned to guarantee such a result. But the young trader, as the challenged, had the right to choose the weapons of Balance, and he *had* chosen...

Wisely. A canny lad, that one. He would do excellently—well. ven'Deelin's very apprentice. How could it be otherwise?

Stinks hammers and starbars, seven paces and closing! We shall have a smash to remember!

Wryly, he looked at his hand, moved his rebuilt arm.

Smash. An apt descriptor, *smash*.

The error then compounded itself, for he might have cried off before ever it came to smashing—his seconds had argued for it, and the boy's second, as well. But, no. By then, he had crossed into that state past anger, long lost to reason. Everything he had wanted in those moments was to kill Jethri Gobelyn ven'Deelin. He had been so enraged that it did not seem possible that he would fail in that goal.

He realized that he had stopped squeezing the ball, and resumed.

Well, he *had* failed. And if he had succeeded, he had no doubt—*now*—that the witnessing crowd would have carried him to the nearest airlock and spaced him. Odd, that the price of both failure and success was the same.

He might have died in truth from failure, had Port Chavvy not proved efficient. There was a wounded man on the docks? Port Chavvy gathered the injured to itself.

Meanwhile, his erstwhile victim, now victor—did not pursue Balance and call the minions of law down upon him. No, the victor, and those who had witnessed the affair—Terrans, very nearly all!—declared that there had been *an accident*, which had left the victor with a head wound, ably doctored by a medic from one of the docked ships, and himself, *smashed.* Questioned, not one deviated from this interpretation of the event, and so did Port Chavvy administration record it.

An accident.

The victim of an accident, he had lived some little while longer, until his mother and his delm had arrived to declare him dead.

He paused, having lost his count, looked down at the ball gripped in his fingers, and began again.

Port Chavvy was situated deep in a backwater spiral arm. It was near to trade lanes menaced by pirates and worlds of chancy circumstance, far from Liad. Liaden culture, tradition—*Liaden law*—meant nothing to Port Chavvy. The notion that a single person might create a death merely by announcing that it was so—that was not a notion to which Port Chavvy subscribed.

Of travelers and crew abandoned by their ships, Port Chavvy was well-versed, and being so far from Liad, and not in the least Liaden, Port Chavvy had fashioned its response to those unfortunates not out of Liaden Balance and questions of *melant'i*, but from the cloth of Terran hospitality.

Port Chavvy, confronted with someone who might bleed to death, stopped the bleeding.

Port Chavvy, confronted with someone who might suicide while despondent and under medication, mounted a watch comprised of volunteers and medics.

Port Chavvy, having seen someone on the path to recovery and judged to no longer present a threat to themselves, provided sleep-learning courses in Terran. Once proficiency was established, Port Chavvy released him to the lower decks and the ARTS halls, first providing ID, a packet including clothing, toiletries, the book, and the number of the wayroom that he would now be pleased to call his home.

When he had been alive, he would have laughed at the idea, but death—death, he discovered, provided a clarifying influence. In fact, he *was* pleased to call this compact and orderly space his home, and—

The door made the high-pitched squeak that meant someone had shown it their ID. It opened to admit Shanna, balancing boxes between hands, and looking practically disheveled.

* * *

Turning into their corridor, Khana saw he was later than he'd thought—the color of the wall was shading subtly from blue to green. When the color was solid, it would be Green Shift. The ARTS—that was, those Awaiting Rescue, Transport or Skilled Habitation—were housed in the older section of Port Chavvy's under-warrens. Five of their nineteen cohabitants were gathered in a wide space designated as "the lounge." It was a gathering place for those who then departed for a group activity, as well as a place to socialize, and the place where the Session was convened.

He had a time or two lingered at the lounge when returning from the Cantina while Bar Jan slept off his pain meds in the early days of their time here, finding it a place where, all being in the ARTS community after all, there was a type of collegiality one might find backstairs at a delm's home, an assumption of being in the same struggle, day by day. His fellow residents had gently corrected his pronunciations, the sleep learner apparently being academic on some words and phrases, not having the local accent, timing, or diction.

There was a corner near the intersection of halls where singers often gathered. This hour, there were five, four engaged in a complex round robin song-sing. All Terran, they nodded, smiled, and allowed him to pass without offering a place to stand. Khana felt a pang. They had used to offer, but he had not once in the twenty-nine days since Bar Jan had been freed from the med wards accepted this extension of that backstairs feeling. Why should the singers continue to open themselves to rebuff?

He continued across the lounge, hurrying now that he realized the time.

"There's the man himself," came a voice from his left, and here was Femta approaching, a meal box in his hand. Khana paused.

Femta rarely spoke, and, having caught Khana's attention, apparently felt no need to speak further. He offered the box, and when Khana did not reach out a hand to accept it, committed himself to a smile.

"Forgive me," Khana said. "I do not. . .understand."

Femta nodded and produced more words.

"Extras from last night. Kitchen help had them boxed, a little care because your friend's been distant. Time they came looking, you'd left, so they asked me to bring them, if you would not mind." The voice was oddly without accent, subdued, unobtrusive, like the person.

"Ah," Khana said, and took a breath. More kindness, he told himself, and offered a smile in return, as he took the additional box.

"Thank you for your care," he said, and added, perhaps not truthfully. "My friend will be grateful."

"No trouble for me," Femta said. "Hope to see your friend out and around soon."

With that, he turned and moved away into the lounge.

Khana shifted his various burdens cautiously. They were a little unwieldy, but it wasn't far now. He continued on his way.

#

A slight figure was turning away from the door to their room as Khana arrived at the top of the hall. Fear spiked, for bounty hunters were not to be discounted, though it had not yet been a relumma, and—

The figure raised her head, and fear evaporated, for it was Joolia, another of their group, so slim and small she appeared Liaden.

The smile she gave him was pure Terran, delight writ large on her pointed face, and touching her dark eyes with warmth.

"There you are!" she said. "I came looking for you, then I didn't want to press the bell, in case your friend was resting."

"Here I am," Khana agreed, smiling in his turn. "Why are you looking for me?"

That was, perhaps, unfortunately phrased. Joolia's face grew solemn.

"I need you—or, well! I need *your help* organizing the common supply room, if you have time? Ferlandy asked me to do it, and I *can* do it, but it'll take some time, it's that messy. So, I need a helper, and I'd seen you that time sorting the lounge closet into order, so quick I don't think anybody else noticed—and I thought—that's who I need for this!"

She looked doubtfully at the boxes in his arms.

"Unless you're busy?"

Khana bowed his head. This, too, reminded of the backstairs, the acknowledgment that one's duty came first but that the sharing of burdens made all lives easier, all more worthy. It was an equality he was amazed to find offered, and was happy to accept.

"I am pleased to assist," he said, "but I must bring my friend his breakfast. I have gotten behind time."

"No worries," Joolia said. "I've got some things to take care of myself. Say we meet at the supply room in an hour, will that do for you? Give us time to do the job and still get to the Session."

"Yes," said Khana, unaccountably warmed. "That will do for me. Thank you."

He moved toward the door, fumbling for the ID card in his jacket pocket. The boxes shifted, and he twisted, making a recover, but—

"Here, let me," said Joolia, dipping a slender hand into his pocket and pulling the ID out. "I'll open the door for you."

She waved the card at the reader, and stepped back as the door began to open. Dropping the card back in his pocket, she turned away.

"I'll see you soon," she said.

#

Within, Bar Jan stood dressed, his good arm visible to what might be a public view, his day slacks on as well as his socks and mocs.

This was good, Khana thought, as he carried the boxes to the table. Occupational Therapy Tech Salmoa had assigned Bar Jan an occupation: to take care of his own needs. True, he should also have been coming to breakfast these last seven days and more, but balanced against that lack was the fact that Bar Jan dressed himself every day, and was meticulous in the exercises meant to strengthen his shattered arm and hand.

That it was difficult for Bar Jan to do these things, Khana had no doubt, for he had seen the sweat on the other man's face.

The exercise was also difficult for Khana, and he had to restrain himself from merely taking the task over. It had been part of his duty, to dress his lord, and to arrange matters, so far as he was able, that his master was in no way impeded in his business.

As he opened the boxes, he recalled his father, who had trained him in his duty, many Standards past: "You must take daily exercise, in order to properly serve. You must be strong, stronger than your lord, though you will never allow him to know it."

There was no doubt who was stronger, now, and that Bar Jan was aware. And how strange it was, that he must now use his strength in support of his master's struggles, and encourage him to do for himself.

"What is all this, Shanna?" Bar Jan was at the table, staring down, the exercise ball held in his spindly fingers. The rest of the arm from shoulder to wrist was still enmeshed in the healing shroud. In public, he wore a white second-hand lab jacket, the front sealed to his throat. In the privacy of their room, he wore a long-sleeved shirt, likewise sealed tightly. Khana pinned both unneeded sleeves neatly out of the way, which was certainly beyond Bar Jan's abilities, no matter his determination, and they both felt the better for it.

"The dinner staff made a box for you. Out of care," he added, because care had not been often present in Bar Jan's life, even between kin.

"Do they think we are desperate?" It seemed that the question was posed in simple curiosity, rather than anger, or insult. Khana was pleased to encourage this mood, so he did not mention that, compared to many on Port Chavvy, they *were* desperate. Instead, he focused on the lesson Miki had given him.

"The kitchen staff, they marked your absence from recent meals, and they felt concern, that your wound was paining you, or that you were unwell, or unhappy. Look, they have sent five of the cheese rolls you favor. The gift is thoughtful."

It was also practical, Khana saw. Each of the cheese rolls was individually wrapped, as were the two dense fiber rolls, with attending jars of jells. The food would keep for days in the carry box.

"So," he finished, looking up to Bar Jan. "These are extra, so that you may follow the tech's advice to *feed yourself up*!"

That of course was said in Terran, the Liaden—even in flexible Low Liaden—being nonsensical.

"I of course strive to follow all of the med tech's excellent advice," Bar Jan said, in a curious flat tone that was neither irony nor pique.

Khana looked at him carefully, before attending the table again. He placed the breakfast box next to the book that Bar Jan kept to hand—the book provided by Port Chavvy to all of its dependents, *Crisis Survivorship: Managing Massive Life Changes*, by Professor Linda Jeef Marteen. The volume was dual-language—Trade and Terran. Khana had read it, but Bar Jan—Bar Jan was *studying* it, performing the various closed and open-eyed meditations from its pages, and sometimes checking a dictionary tablet, that usually with a scowl.

"You are behind on your meal," Khana said. "Eat now, and I will tell you the news before I must go to an—" He paused, unsure of how to describe the task for which Joolia had requested his assistance—"an appointment."

"An appointment," still that odd, uninflected tone. Bar Jan put the ball aside, and sat to table. Spork in hand, he looked up.

"Shanna, may I have my ID card?"

"Certainly!" He pulled it from his pocket and placed it atop the book.

"My thanks." Bar Jan murmured. "So, there is news?"

"The comet continues our way," Khana began. "The station is attempting a protocol to increase our margin of safety. This from the newsboard. The audit of the meteor shields has been completed. It seems that they are more vulnerable than anticipated to the unique threat of this comet, which has both density and mass as well as velocity and rotation. The combination of these might breach the shields."

Khana paused, but Bar Jan seemed utterly intent on his meal.

"A number of ships at dock have filed for early departure, one assumes from concerns regarding the comet's pass."

"They will be safer undocked, if the station is struck," Bar Jan said, with something like his old authority. Khana blinked, and then recalled that he had been fascinated by the practical business of ships, which his mother and delm had deplored.

"Is there other news?" Bar Jan asked, glancing up from his meal.

"Ah! There is indeed. The Port has increased the ARTS allotments. Base rate increases eight percent; medical stipend increases six percent; the volunteer rate increases by four percent; facilitators will receive a one percent increase."

"Eight percent—" Bar Jan had always been good at his numbers. Now, he lifted his eyebrows, doing, so Khana supposed, sums in his head.

"You might achieve your own suite, Shanna."

He had not thought of that, and he paused to do so before shrugging it aside.

"What I had thought," he said, as Bar Jan finished his meal and closed the box, "is that we might together achieve a larger space. I daresay that will be best for both of us."

"Yes, you *do* dare say," Bar Jan answered--angry words, but there was no heat in his voice. "Always planning, Shanna, and giving direction."

Seated as he was, Khana bowed, his temper engaged by this flat-voiced accusation. In all the years he had served Bar Jan chel'Gaiban, he had never felt such anger as this. It would have been inappropriate, given their *melant'is.*

But here, where there was no *melant'i*, no *Code*–

"Indeed, yes, I gave direction, and was sometimes fortunate to see you accept it!" The voice was hard--*angry*. It was a moment before Khana realized that it was *his* voice, and by that time he was sweeping on.

"When you bothered to take my direction, you wore the proper suit at the proper time, the proper shoes, and boots. When you bothered to take my direction, your mother noticed you with more favor and less anger. I directed your choices, from hair shine to socks, for that was my duty! As for planning--only see the success of *your* planning! You might have died in truth, save for *my* planning, *my* direction, *my* appeal—"

He stopped, his breath caught in horror. Bar Jan was standing, he saw, and realized that he was, as well.

There was a way to heal this, Khana thought rapidly. He need only admit his error, abase himself, and speak mildly.

He took a careful breath, averting his eyes.

"Master--" he began--and stopped, because Bar Jan had raised his good hand.

He was in pain, Khana saw, marking the damp forehead, the tight mouth, the narrowed eyes. He was too frail for. . .

Bar Jan sighed softly. "I have waited too long for this," he said. "It must be acknowledged, and it is mine to do."

He took a deep, deliberate breath, and in that moment the cheap station clothes were the business attire of a lord; a man of substance and *melant'i*.

Then, he bowed.

It was. . .a simple bow, carefully flensed of years of hauteur. It was a bow Khana had never in his years of duty seen from one of Rinork, much less from the heir himself.

It was the bow between equals, with an additional careful tip of the head, which acknowledged that a debt was owed.

Face grim, Bar Jan straightened, waiting.

"Yes," Khana managed against a tight throat.

His bow was simple as well. The bow between equals, with the hand sign that conveyed all debts were paid.

He paused, resisting another bow, and instead closed on Bar Jan, clapping him on his good shoulder, as an equal might after a game of *piket*.

"Come, let me check your wrappings, and then I must to my appointment. Will you come to the Session today?"

Bar Jan hesitated as he turned to the chair.

"I--will be reading," he said after a moment.

Khana paused with his hand on med box, wondering if he dared to push again.

Well, and why not?

"The boy at the Cantina--Miki--asked after your health and professes that he will be pleased to see you again. Our. . .neighbors here, as well. They ask of you, of your health. They care for you."

Improbably, Bar Jan's face relaxed into a smile.

"No, Shanna," he said gently. "They care for *you*."

TWO

Joolia was already at work when Khana arrived, having made a start of clearing the counters on the right side of the room. She had removed the hooded over-garment she wore in the hallways and the lounge, and rolled the sleeves of the sweater beneath. There was a look of grim determination on her pointed face that reminded him of Bar Jan.

She turned as he entered the room, grimness melting into a faint smile.

"You came!"

"Of course I came," he answered, remembering to answer her smile. "Did I not say so?"

"Well, you did, but I wouldn't've much blamed you, if you'd taken one look at this mess and just backed out."

Khana looked about him.

Yes, he thought, *mess* would cover it.

"What happened?" he asked. He had been in the common supply room many times, to draw clean towels, recyclable dishes, cutlery--and while it always had the slightly disheveled look of a space that was used briefly by many individuals, it had never been this. . .chaotic.

Joolia sighed.

"Cazzy had the Scareds come on her over sleep-shift. Hasn't happened for a long time, Windy said. I've never seen it, but I haven't been here so long. Anyhow, the Scareds make her think there's something hiding and waiting to get her, an' last night I guess she s'posed whatever it was, it was hiding in here."

She blew out a breath, turning in place to survey the carnage.

"Anyway, Ferlandy an' Windy caught her at it, only not too soon, as you can see, and took her up to the clinic. Windy came back with Ferlandy's word could I set things to right, so here *I* am. Then I got a good look, figured I needed help, and here *you* are."

"I am," Khana agreed, "and the two of us will soon put it right."

She smiled again. "You sound like somebody who knows what he's doing. Since I don't, that makes you lead. Tell me what and how and I'll do it."

Khana saw what she had done so far and what needed done.

"First, we will separate those things which must go into the recycler and those that are still whole and useful."

"Right you are," Joolia said. "I'll take this side."

Joolia was a determined worker, and Khana had Standards of experience in sorting out messes of all kinds. Between them, the first step was quickly accomplished.

"Whew," Joolia said, as they paused for a moment to survey their progress. "I'd never have gotten this far, this fast, without you, Khana."

"Why did Ferlandy give you the task? If asking does not offend."

She laughed.

"Well, see, I'm a research librarian, and in Ferlandy's thinking, a librarian is somebody who keeps things in order so other people can find them."

Khana blinked, wondering—

"Ah," he said, enlightened. "Ferlandy makes no difference between righting chaos and keeping order."

"That's it." She gave him an approving nod. "But you--where'd you learn to find order in a mess?"

"A subset of my training," he said, surveying what remained for them. Cazzy had been thorough, and most of what had been in the cabinets now--was not. Fortunately, the closets were labeled, which would make the next stage of their operation much easier. There was a system in place, even if it was a system that Khana itched to adjust; they would not be slowed down, by having to invent their own.

"Training in what? If it's not an insult to ask," Joolia said.

He turned to face her.

"I. . .was," he said slowly, "a *kie'floran*, which required me to care for the personal belongings of. . .the one I served, to pack, unpack, to always know where everything was, and put it away into its proper place when it was no longer needed. As much as possible also to be sure of the timing of things, to aid with the meeting of appointments and necessities."

"And your friend?" she asked, then quickly brought her hand to her lips. "I'm sorry, that's prying. Only, I was thinking, if Ferlandy knew what his training was, maybe there was something he--your friend--could be set to do. Which would help him feel better." Color stained her cheekbones, and he realized that she, like Miki before her, had been discomfited by her own boldness.

"Of course," she said, her voice strained. "He might not be well enough. . ."

Khana glanced at the wall. They were approaching time for the Session. If they wished to be done ordering the room by then, they had best move on.

"The next step," he said, stretching his arms out to encompass the room, "is to create piles of like and like." He looked around. Cazzy had not been dainty in her search for assassins. "I suggest we use the table."

"All right," Joolia said, sounding somewhat subdued. She bent and gathered an armful of miscellaneous items to carry to the worktable.

Khana brought his armful to the opposite end, and began to work. The song from the group at the intersection of the hallways was suddenly very loud. He looked up from his sorting, and his glance crossed Joolia's. Sighing somewhat, he answered her question as best he was able.

"My friend," he said, slowly. "He was trained to be the center--unchanging, fixed--and to also seek advantage—for himself, and for those who were aligned with him. He had not a trade, such as you have, or I, but a *position*."

He glanced up. Joolia's head was down, watching her own hands. He left the table to gather more items for sorting, and fell into the rhythm of the work.

When Joolia spoke again, he started, and looked up to meet her eyes.

"So," she said. "He doesn't know who he is, anymore, with all that gone--all those people and systems that he was center for."

Khana cleared his throat.

"Yes," he said. "Exactly that. It is--hard for him."

"I'm guessing so," said Joolia, giving him a faint smile. "But he looks sharp, yanno? He'll figure himself out."

"Yes," said Khana, his throat unaccountably tight. "I am certain that he will."

A thought occurred then, and he raised a hand.

"You are a research librarian," he said.

"That's right." The smile was broader this time. "Got something you need researched? I owe you for your help, after all."

He had previously noticed that some Terrans practiced an informal sort of Balance, and it pleased him that Joolia was one of them.

"Yes, if you please," he said. "I wonder if you could find for me what the word *Jeef* means."

* * *

Bar Jan re-read the chapters on decision-making and self-management. The book would have one select for personal happiness, rather than advantage, which was not at all a Liaden concept, but one he thought he might adopt. Considering happiness, he made a cup of tea, and unwrapped one of the cheese rolls.

His happiness had never been of much importance to anyone, including himself. He was the son of Rinork, heir to her honors and her duties. If he had thought of the matter in the terms provided by the book, he would have realized that those things did not make him happy; that his duties weighed heavily on him; that the constant seeking of advantage made him—angry.

He had been happy, he realized now, when the pilots and mechanics would speak to him of ship lore and the mysteries of piloting, though he had gained no advantage from their lessons. In fact, the opposite, for his mother had despised him for his interest. Why did he bother himself? she had asked. He was plainly no pilot, nor ever would be. Perhaps, she had suggested caustically, he proposed to be a mechanic?

But no. It was unthinkable that one of Rinork, never mind the heir, might study to become a spaceship mechanic.

No matter; his current situation also put that. . .potential. . .happiness out of reach.

Sipping tea, he stared through the wall and into the past.

What else, then, he asked himself.

Had it made him happy to ruin livelihoods, and tarnish reputations? Would he have been *happy*, if he had killed Jethri Gobelyn ven'Deelin?

He suspected not, even if he had managed to survive the act.

Well, then. Was he so poor a thing that he had no happiness in him?

There must, he thought, feeling his chest tighten in something like the old panic--there must be *some*thing since his death that had caused him to feel, if not happiness, then--contentment?

Malvern. The thought rose so sudden and so certain that he sat, amazed, until his mind began to work again. Then, he followed the steps outlined in the book, to discover whether it was Malvern herself—her person, her demeanor—which gave him ease; some aspect of the environment in which she operated, or--

It came in a flash: The first time Shanna had bullied him into walking to the Cantina to claim and eat his breakfast. There had been Malvern, clearly in command of the enterprise. She had taken note of them—of him in particular as he stood puzzling over the breads and sweet things on offer. She had taken time to go over every item with him, making certain he understood the nature of each, correcting his faltering Terran with neither mockery nor patronage. He had been happy—in her company, in the lore she had shared, and especially in her parting comment, that, once his arm was healed, he might if he wished take up an apprenticeship, and learn how to bake.

He had regarded that pleasantry as a *promise*, he realized now. He had kept it close, giving himself something to look forward to that was not the pills he had hidden away against a time when surcease from pain was all he had left.

Bar Jan finished the roll, and the tea, considering his next step. The book would have him make a list of things that stood between him and his happiness, and another list, of how he would surmount each.

To make that list, he needed the assistance of an expert. He would, he thought, standing, go to the Cantina and find Malvern, else her second, and learn what he needed to do in order to become a baker.

He would go. Now.

* * *

Joolia closed the last cabinet and stood with her palms against the door as if she expected the towels inside to come rushing out at her.

"Done," she said, after a moment, and turned around to give Khana a grin.

"Done," he agreed, "and in good time. Listen. The singing has stopped."

"Well, then, it's us for the Session, my friend! We can make a report of progress."

She pushed the sleeves of her sweater down, took up her hooded jacket and slipped it on.

Khana turned slowly on his heel, surveying the room. All was seemly. Good. He smiled, pleased.

"It does feel good, doesn't it," Joolia said from beside him. "Looking at it now, and remembering how it had been?"

"Yes," he said, turning his head to smile at her. "You worked well."

"I just did what I was told. Couldn't've gone nearly as well without you breaking it all down into steps for me." She jerked her head toward the door. "C'mon, let's grab some good seats."

She turned and went out into the hall, Khana one step behind her. At the entrance to the lounge, he paused, and turned toward their room—

And found his arm caught in a surprisingly firm grip.

"Hey," said Joolia, "the Session's this way."

Khana opened his mouth, and she shook her head.

"He'll be OK," she said. "If he wants to come to the Session, he will. Right?"

Khana considered her with something like wonder.

"Right," he said, and followed her into the lounge.

#

The Session was unlike any other event Khana had attended in his previous life. The first meeting had been horrifying; the second bewildering, but by the end of the third, he'd become accustomed.

It was the one dependable marker in days that were sometimes too much alike. Attendance was not compulsory, but most ARTS did attend. Khana made it a point to come to every meeting, bringing Bar Jan when he could manage it, which had not been often.

A Liaden would say that the purpose of the Session was to publicly display one's vulnerabilities, surely a risky endeavor.

Now at this, his tenth Session, Khana was comfortable with—and comforted by—the Progress Report, and hoped one day to have something to share, himself.

Chairs were arranged in the lounge in a semi-circle facing a table at which the leader stood. Everyone took turns as leader, and Khana realized with a start that *he* would have a turn, if he attended eight out of the next ten Sessions.

Today, Femta stood at the table, waiting while seats filled.

"Got only one item of general bidness today," he said when the talk had subsided. "Cazzy's at clinic. Ferlandy's with her. He sends she'll be took down to the planet for treatment, if the clinic techs can't figure out a new good dose for to keep her easy. Anybody wants to stop by and catch up, now's the time."

He paused for a slow count of ten. When no one stood, or spoke, he nodded.

"This Session is a joint meeting of Travelers Awaiting Rescue, Transport or Skilled Habitation and Port Chavvy Residents Accepting Aid. We convene every two days to report our efforts to improve Port Chavvy however we may, and to fortify our own lives and well-being by sharing our searches for increased prosperity for all."

That was the formal start of every Session, followed by, "Success and failure may be equally discussed, because as we all know—progress is a history of failures gone right."

Femta looked at those assembled, took one step back from the table and opened his arms, as if he would embrace all who were gathered.

"Who's seen progress or caught a success?"

"I have!" A plump woman in overalls embroidered with strange flowers stood up. Khana recognized her as one of the singers.

"Boradeen," she said, at Femta's nod. "Four and a half Standards ART. Just got the confirm—tomorrow I'm reporting to Air Filtration Nine, to start training for backup tech."

There was was a whistle from the back row of chairs. Somebody upfront clapped.

Boradeen grinned.

"Really," she said, grinning, "pretty much what I did on Sylvester's cruise ships, 'cept there I was running a whole stinks crew—pretty much ASO—All Shifts On! Here it'll be a five hour shift every five days, working on units I'm half familiar with. Chance to move up. Gimme a Standard and I'll be off the hall."

"Don't you go too far, too fast, Bordy, we need you on the quartets!"

There was laughter—and a sudden solemn look on the singer's face.

"True," she said. "I just got some of you trained right. Prolly they'll keep me alt-shift for awhile, so I won't be missing practs too soon."

There was a smattering of claps as she sat down, still smiling.

"Right, then," Femta said. "Who else?"

Windy stood. In Khana's experience, Windy spoke second at every meeting, and he always had a piece of hardcopy in his hand, which he would look at, rather than at those gathered.

The last time Khana had seen Windy at the Session, he had wept during his entire presentation, as had several other members of the meeting.

Today, Windy was dressed in a light blue lab coat, kin to Bar Jan's white one. Not new, either garment, but not shabby.

"Windy VinHalin, two Standards and nine-tens on Port. My aunt Mithes, she's back in 'hab for too much 'stim, but she got my news to her youngest sister. That's Cindra, some of you might recall. Cindra, she sent some credit toward clothes—" He caught his sleeve in his free hand and raised his arms, showing off his finery.

When he lowered his arms, he stared at the hardcopy for a long time, then looked up, at Femta, who nodded.

"Right," Windy said, sounding breathless. "So Cindra, she—it says in her letter she's going to court to force the Chaendle Line trustees to make good on my ticket."

Someone cheered, but Windy waved him down.

"First date she's got is for a circuit court—judge comes in start of next Standard. Meantime, the advocate, she thinks they might raise me a ticket if the funds ain't spooled by then. That'd be two Standards, with the orbits all running together."

He looked back at the hardcopy, and told it, "So, I'm here for a bit yet, even with best luck."

The groan was universal, accompanied by shaking heads, muttered curses, and frustrated sighs.

"That's progress," Windy said, voice firm, and sat down.

Khana felt a light pressure against his arm. He turned his head, but Joolia was already rising.

"Joolia Tenuta. One Standard even, come tomorrow blue shift. I've got pick-up work at Port Admin, doing law and precedent research. Might go somewhere interesting, though I'm still hoping for a ship."

She paused to look down at him, and tugged on his arm. Belatedly understanding, Khana stood.

"Ferlandy asked me to clean up the mess that overtook the common supply area. I realized it was too big for me, so I asked Khana for an assist. He took lead, and the result is the room's back in good order."

She looked at him. He looked at her.

"You got anything to add, Khana?" Femta asked, kindly.

Khana touched tongue to lips.

"It was a pleasure to assist," he said, faintly. And the room erupted into whistles and claps.

* * *

He had taken a wrong turn, and then another in an attempt to correct his course. Still, he eventually came to his intended location, if somewhat later into the Port-day than he had supposed he would. This was, he reminded himself, as he rested on a bench outside the Cantina's entrance, not a failure, but a success. He had achieved Step One of his Action Plan: Arrive at the Cantina.

Step Two was: Enter the Cantina and speak with Malvern about his Goal, asking her advice in how best to achieve it. If Malvern was not present, he would identify the next most knowledgeable person on staff and speak with them. He would proceed to that step as soon as he was rested. It would not help his case if he arrived breathless and disordered. A calm face was necessary.

As he sat, resting, he reviewed his Plan in its entirety, especially the necessity to thank whomever he found to advise him, even if they had not been useful to his Goal. *Immediately useful*, he corrected himself, to *this* Goal. He might, after all, have a new Goal, later, and again require advice.

Also, he thought, he should make another Plan, which was to have something to eat and drink while he was in the Cantina, so that the walk. . .home would be easier.

He took a breath, assessing himself, finding that he was rested and calm. Excellent. On to Step Two.

#

There were no diners in the Cantina. Behind the counter was someone he had never seen before.

"Help you?" she asked, smiling.

He smiled, and came to the counter. "Thank you," he said, in Terran, because that was courtesy. "Is Malvern here?"

She shook her head. "She's been called up, hon. We're doing the best we can without her."

He was not clear on *called up*, though he grasped the general message was that Malvern was not present—but for how long?

"She will return?" he asked.

Her face altered, though he wasn't sure of the meaning of this new expression.

"Sure, she'll be back, don't you worry about that! We just don't know when. Hoping for soon. Is there somebody else can help you now?"

He had thought of this, and prepared his next question.

"The one who performs Malvern's duties, in absence? Is that one here?" He paused, thought, and added, "I need advice."

The smile was back.

"Well, we all kinda split Malvern's job stuff between us, 'cause it's four of us to one of her. The second-key-holder, though—Acting

Manager—that's Baydee, and she's right in the back. I'll go get her for you. Wait right there."

She vanished through the door that he supposed led to the kitchens, and he stood where he was. He heard voices, faint, then footsteps. The door swung open, and a woman he recalled from his few previous visits to the Cantina emerged. She was younger than Malvern, shorter, and rounder. Her hair was bundled under a white cap, and she wore an apron. There was a smear of pale dust—perhaps flour—on one dark cheek.

"Hey," she said, with a nod. She came to the counter and leaned her arms on it. "I'm Baydee. You're Khana's friend, right? I remember you were in a couple times. What can I do for you?"

"I wish to become a—baker, or, more. A chef. Like yourself. I hoped you could give me advice. . .how I would achieve this."

She considered him, eyes inevitably going to his damaged arm. He recruited himself to wait.

"I'm taking this is a long-term goal," Baydee said finally.

He was pleased. She understood.

"Yes, thank you. If there is study, or work that I could begin now, as I heal, or—" He moved his good hand in the gesture he had seen others use to signify the depth of their ignorance.

"Gotcha. Can I see your ticket?"

He hesitated, which was foolish. He had asked for advice, and Baydee was the current expert willing to give him advice. She was not going to rob him of his ID.

He took it from his pocket and offered it across the palm of his undamaged hand.

"'K, now. . ." Baydee squinted slightly as she read the card, then nodded and handed it back.

"So, there's some details you need to tend to before you can start working on your goal." She gave him a smile. "Stuff that you can work on while you're waiting for your arm to finish healing."

Ah, this was excellent! He inclined his head, recalled himself, and said, "Please go on."

"Right. Now, first thing is you still got a Port Chavvy general ticket—what I mean to say is that it's coded with your number, but there's no name. You wanna start contributing to the station's welfare, you gotta do it under your name." He stirred and she held up a hand.

"Hear me out. It don't have to be whatever your name is, Out from here, but it does have to be a name you'll answer to, and that you'll care enough about to keep it outta trouble. So, first thing's to line up what you want people to call you, and file that with the Port right now, if you're so minded." She nodded toward something that was apparently over his shoulder. He turned, looked, and saw the public terminal in the corner.

"Thank you," he said. "It is a fact that my. . .former name must give way to another." And soon, he reminded himself silently; before the grace period was run and Rinork sent bounty hunters to deal with nameless rogues posing as chel'Gaibin.

Baydee gave him an approving nod. "That's right. New beginnings. You can get the new name set up while you're still on medical, but you can't volunteer or 'prentice til you're off medical." She raised a hand again, though he had not been about to speak.

"You be sensible and wait til the medics let you go. There'll be hungry people to feed when you got two good arms to feed 'em with, and you don't wanna stop once you start, so make sure the medics *clear you*, right?"

"Right," he said, seriously.

"Once you're cleared, you can apply for volunteer, and even 'prentice. You'll prolly hafta wait for something to come open, so you work at general volunteer, like we all do, and you hook yourself into the Port's vocational library and start educating yourself, and maybe fine tune your goal. What you said right at first? You wanted to be a baker—a chef? Those are two different things, so you'll want to get clear about which is it, or—" Another smile. "Might turn out that it's something else—that's OK, too. Goals change."

"I am—grateful," he said, and that was honest. "You have given me—"

"Be aware and awake, Cantina! Klyken is here!"

Following the shout came a tall, extremely thin man wearing a bouffant white hat, and spotless white tunic, trousers, and shoes.

"Baydee!" he cried. "I will inform myself, and then we will bake!"

"Yessir," Baydee said, but Klyken had already swept through the door into the kitchen. He could be heard calling for station reports. Baydee smiled.

"Looks like I'm on. You need anything else before I go?"

"I should eat. . ." he began, and stopped as the door came open at Baydee's back and Klyken stepped up to the counter.

"I met you," he said pointing at the damaged arm with his first finger—a rudeness to Liadens, but he reminded himself that he was no longer Liaden.

"Yes," Klyken continued, "before this thing happened with your arm. You came to my restaurant with a large party from *Wynhael*. You had the three cheese soup, the hunion bread, and a stripe of beefsta, rare. Also, my nillon crisp-crust stuffed with whirled berry spread. It appeared you enjoyed it very much."

It was so very distant, that memory, but he *did* remember the meal, even as he chose not to recall why his mother had gathered those particular people to dine with them.

"It was a fine meal, one of the best I recall enjoying," he said to Klyken, and it wasn't a lie. "You are the chef at the Long View Restaurant?"

"Chef-owner," Klyken said, and there was pride—justified—in his voice and face.

He shook his head then.

"It would be good to talk with you, about memorable meals, hey? But I am here to bake Malvern's special dark, and train Baydee and Miki in the way of it. If you are here to find a meal, please continue, and we will send out to finish the—"

"I am here," he heard himself say, "because I wished to learn what I must do to become a baker, or a chef. Baydee has given me much good advice. But, I would—is it possible to watch you at work?"

There was silence. He swallowed, wondering if—knowing that—he had overstepped.

Baydee spoke. "He's on medical."

"Hah. So, he is disallowed from volunteering or standing as a 'prentice." Klyken looked him in the eye. "Have you ever seen bread made? Have you made bread, or any other foodstuff for others to eat?"

"No," he said, his mouth dry.

"So. What you know is that you like to eat. What you need to discover is whether you like to cook."

"Yes," he said, very nearly voiceless.

"You may watch," Klyken said. He looked at Baydee. "We all understand that he is neither volunteer nor 'prentice. He is allowed to watch because I have said it."

"Right," Baydee said.

Klyken turned and vanished through the door into the kitchens.

Baydee waved him down counter, and opened the pass-through.

"Come on back, and let's find you a good spot for to watch."

* * *

"Well, but see, there's where your math's gone off. If it was a simple *comet*, you'd be solid, not sayin' not, but that thing ain't no more a wild comet than I am. That's runaway mining, that's what that is—a broke off piece of that planetary mining op they just up and left—you remember that! That's why Chavvy Admin thought they could steer it away, 'cause they was sending 'structions to the rigs still attached. Not a bad idea, but no word if it worked, an' if it don't work—"

Khana sat between Bordy and the person introduced as Malc, with whom Bordy was speaking. Loudly. Joolia was across the table and three places to the right, in earnest conversation with a man in a bright green volunteers vest.

He wasn't quite sure how he had gotten caught up into the group, but here he was in a public diner near station center, many halls removed from the wayrooms, having ordered his food, and presented his ID, which was accepted with neither comment nor smile.

"Well, it din't work," a new voice said, as a thump sounded just behind and to Khana's left. He turned his head and saw a man in a Port Chavvy foreman's uniform straddling a chair, his arms folded on the back. His face was damp, and drawn.

"Hey, Reg," Bordy said, not so loudly.

On Khana's other side, Malc turned his head. He paused, then lifted his arm.

"Reg needs a beer, here, mate! Put 'er 'gainst the mercy fund!"

"Comin' up!" came an answering shout.

"What din't work?" Bordy asked.

"Contacting the machinery on that hunk o'asteroid bearing down on us—preciate it," this last to the woman who delivered a bulb of dark liquid to his hand. He took a moment to drink, sighed, and shook his head.

"Well, we got the machine's attention, all right. Then we sent that it should move itself to the coords the pilots'd worked out. An' it tried. Looked like it was gonna work for a couple minutes, there."

He paused for another gulp from the bulb.

"Problem wasn't the idea, or the machine. Problem was the rock being unstable. Protoplanets are like that, half random and all. Enough frozen gas, mixed salts, and wanna-be ocean to make things interesting. Enough to spout off like a comet, dense enough to hit hard if it hits something. They'd had the rig all tied and gridded in for the long haul, but the machine moved, and it—blooie!—fragmented."

Silence.

Out of the corner of his eye, Khana saw Joolia rise from her place and leave the table, apparently headed for the screen in the back corner of the room.

"Soooo," Bordy extended the word as if she were singing it, "what's that mean, zackly?"

Reg finished what was left in the bulb. Somebody reached over his shoulder and took it out of his hand. There were, Khana saw, quite a number of people gathered 'round, listening with worry plain on their faces.

"What it means, zackly, is that we got some luck, but not too much." Reg straightened and looked around him, noting those listening, and nodding his head.

"See, the big rock, it broke into three pieces, mostly, with some odd crumbs here and there. The biggest piece, with the machine attached, looks like that's gonna fly on by, big miss, now that all other stuff got flung off by rotation.

"Second piece is small enough, it'll prolly stick with the big one, even though they ain't connected any more. If it does separate, it'll still miss us."

"An' the third piece?" Malc asked.

Reg sighed.

"Well, now the third piece—no machinery attached, but it's a sizeable rock all on its own, with some gas and ice to boot. Really pretty when you look at it through a lens, yanno? Just like a regular comet!"

He shook his head.

"The third piece—buncha that's gonna hit us, friends. Real soon now."

* * *

He stood outside of the Cantina, trying to pull his dazzled wits together. What he had witnessed—it had been. . .enthralling. The discipline, the grace, the inevitability of the loaves. It had been an honor, to observe. It had been . . .a great happiness, to eat a slice of the first loaf, still warm from the oven.

While the baking went forward, he had been allowed to assist in the inventory of supplies, so that Baydee could place her order with Supply. His attendance upon Baydee had allowed Miki to do the day's accounting and file receipts with Finance. Therefore, he had been useful.

There at last being nothing else for him to do, he had taken his leave, and now stood by the bench, recruiting himself.

"Well, my friend," a lately familiar voice said from near at hand, "and how do you find the making of food?"

He turned, his body inclining by itself into a small bow of respect.

"I find it compelling and good," he said. "I will wish to pursue this, I think."

"Do you? It is not an easy trade, but it has compensations." There was a pause as Klyken came beside him.

"I don't want to offend, but, why do you stand here?"

"I am trying to recall the route home," he said, though admitting his uncertainty would give Klyken an advantage over him. "I became confused on my way here, and I would avoid making the same error."

"No, better by far to make new errors," Klyken said, with a smile. "You are in the ARTS halls?"

"Yes."

"If you like, we can walk together for a while, and I will point you the rest of the way to your halls when we part."

He had just given Klyken an advantage over him, old habit said. Would he now put himself into his hands?

This had been covered in the book, that old habits might arise and lead to action inappropriate to a new situation. It took time to form new, more appropriate habits, thus mindfulness was suggested.

He took a deep breath, and smiled at Klyken.

"That would be most kind of you," he said.

#

Klyken spoke, after they turned the first corner

"Your ship left you, I heard. Family emergency they said. Always sad, such things."

He continued to walk, and said nothing, ignoring the clamoring of old habit in the back of his head.

"They left me, too," said the chef without rancor, "with bills for five banquets unpaid."

"I. . .regret," he said, when Klyken paused.

"Eh." The other man shrugged. "I filed a claim with the Port. If *Wynhael* comes back, she must pay my bill, and interest, before she can dock." A pause. "Do you know if *Wynhael* will come back? For you, maybe?"

Almost, he laughed, but Klyken was Terran, and would not understand his reasons. He said, gently.

"No, Master Klyken, *Wynhael* will *not* come back for me."

Klyken made a soft sound, and spoke again.

"I heard that you were the son of the trader, and that she threw you away."

He said nothing. What was there to say? After a few steps Klyken continued.

"It isn't a good thing, to throw a child away. I know that I have been sorry, for a long time now."

They walked on, turning another corner, and continuing down a hallway that seemed to him familiar.

"I regret," he said again, and indeed he felt sadness for the master's obvious sorrow.

"Eh." Klyken shrugged again. "The Long View—my restaurant. That is my child, now."

They turned another corner, and Klyken stopped. He did, too, turning to look at the chef.

"This is where we part," Klyken said, and raised his arm to point. "You—you walk straight down this hall until that intersection, where the news screen is, eh? At that intersection, you turn right, then continue straight ahead. Another two hall crossings and you will be home."

"Thank you," he said. "I hope to see you again."

"For that, I hope you will come up to the Long View when the medics free you. I often need an extra worker, and I've seen tonight that you know how to work."

He felt tears prick his eyes.

"I will come," he said.

"I'll look forward to that," said Klyken, and with that turned, walking back to the intersection, and taking the left-hand hall.

He stood another moment to compose himself, and began to smile, recalling again the Cantina, the bread, the inventory! Smiling, he walked down the familiar hallway, toward home.

* * *

The walls were purple when Khana returned to the wayrooms with Bordy, and Windy, and Joolia. Malc had come along, too, though he wasn't a resident. Bordy had asked Reg to come with them, but he'd shaken his head, and said something about telling Ferlandy to expect a call up.

Khana hadn't noted the passage of time, but, now they were home, and the wall was purple, and Bar Jan—

He gasped.

"Khana?" Joolia said. "Something wrong?"

"My. . .friend. . .I should not have left him so long."

She looked serious. "He that frail he can't be left? I mean, I know he's still on medical, but—"

"Who's up for a game of Corners?" Bordy called. "Khana?"

"No, I thank you," he managed. "It is late, and I must. . .go home."

Bordy grinned. "Did get a little long, din't it? Well, some time other, then."

Khana smiled, but he was already moving toward his corridor, their small room. Bar Jan. . .There was a hoard of pills, he was certain of it, though he had never found them. If Bar Jan had thought himself abandoned—abandoned *again*. . .

It was then that he realized Joolia was still with him.

He looked at her in surprise. She shrugged.

"In case you need help," she said. "'less you'd rather I leave?"

"No. . ." he said, which was the truth, as he reached into his pocket, pulled out the ID, and waved it at the reader.

The door slid out of the way. He stepped through, leaving Joolia behind as he went swiftly through the tiny 'fresher, returning to the main room to stare around the painfully neat space.

The painfully neat and *empty* space.

There on the table was Bar Jan's book, the medical supplies, and a notetaker. The extra rolls from the morning were not on the table, but they might have equally been placed in the cool box, or taken as wander-food.

"Wander-food," he repeated aloud, mocking himself. Where was there to wander, on a space station?

"Problem?" Joolia asked.

He blinked at her.

"He is not here, and that is not like him. He does not. . .care to leave the room."

"Might've gone out to get something to eat?" Joolia suggested. "It's late, but if he's not used to goin' about by himself, he might've got lost. Where would he most likely go?"

"The Cantina," Khana said, and felt a shudder of guilt. In the other events of the day, he had forgotten to tell Bar Jan that Malvern had been marked by the Port for duty. He forced himself to think. What Joolia suggested made sense. Bar Jan was not accustomed to going about by himself, and there were several sections between home and the Cantina where the confluence of the hallways required interpretation.

Khana started toward the door.

"I will go and see if I can find him," he said to Joolia, as he opened the door, and started back up the corridor. "Thank you."

"No worries. I'll go with you, if you want."

He looked at her again.

"Yes," he said. "Thank you."

Together they crossed the Lounge, ignoring the card players in the far corner, and came out into the public hall at the intersection where the singers gathered during day-shifts.

Khana turned left, which was the only choice, from the wayrooms. At the next intersection, however, he would have to decide if Bar Jan would have attempted the twisty back halls, or kept to the more public ways.

They were only steps away from that intersection, when a thin man with bright golden hair, one sleeve of his white coat pinned up, turned the corner.

"Shanna!" cried Bar Jan, flinging up his good arm.

He stopped, staring, thinking for a moment that Bar Jan was. . .glowing. But no, he was standing in the subtle spill of light from a night dim, that was all.

"Where have you been?" he asked. "I came back and you were gone."

"Then we are both keeping late hours," Bar Jan said jovially—*jovially*. "Shanna, I hope your adventure was as amazing as mine."

"It was—very pleasant," Khana said, and felt his stomach clench as Bar Jan turned toward Joolia.

"Hello," he said. "I have seen you, but it is my error that I do not know your name."

"Joolia Tenuta," she said. "I'm glad you're home. Khana was—" she broke off, and turned.

"He calls you Shanna?"

"Yes," said Bar Jan before he could speak. "I was a small boy when I. . .met Khana, and could not say his name properly. It is his kindness that he has never corrected me."

Joolia smiled. "It's a nickname. I get it. You've known each other a long time, then?"

"Yes," Bar Jan said. "When we met, I had not quite eight Standards."

"I had fourteen," Khana said, and added, for what reason he could not have said. "I now have twenty-nine."

Joolia's eyes widened.

"All that time together, you're practically brothers," she said, and touched Khana lightly on the sleeve. "Hey, that word you wanted to know what it means—*jeef*?"

Bar Jan went still.

"Yes?" said Khana.

"So I took a minute while everybody was being noisy at the meal, and put a search in to the central library through the public terminal. Picked it up when we were leaving." He'd seen her get up and leave the group table, Khana recalled.

"Turns out that *jeef*? It don't mean anything in Terran, Trade, or Liaden. Prolly a name-word."

"Professor Linda Jeef Marteen," Bar Jan said quietly. "Joolia Tenuta, please explain about names. Is it permitted that I. . .use a name of an admired person as my own? Or do I. . .steal from them?"

"Oh, *you* wanted to know!" Joolia turned to him. "So long's you're only using a piece—you're not planning on setting up as Professor Linda Jeef Marteen, are you? Pretending to be her, is what I mean."

There was a small pause, which Khana knew was Bar Jan deciphering Joolia's question.

"No," he said at last. "I wish to call myself Jeef before the Port. I was advised to choose a name that I care enough about to *keep it out of trouble*." That was said very carefully—a quote, Khana thought, from Bar Jan's advisor. "I have admiration for Professor Marteen—her book, the process of her thought. I would honor her, and remind myself of. . .who I am, now."

"Don't see any problem with that," Joolia said. "You're still on medical?"

"Yes. I was advised that I could register a name while on medical."

"That's right, you can. There's a form. You want somebody to stand by while you're filling it out, in case you got a question, I'll volunteer for that. I'm a librarian, so I pretty much got forms down."

Another pause before Bar Jan gave a measured nod of his head, not quite a bow.

"Thank you," he said. "I will be. . .glad of your help."

There was another pause before Joolia cleared her throat.

"When do you think you'll be ready to make the change?"

Bar Jan's eyebrows went up. "Now," he said, definitely, and glanced aside. "Shanna? You also, I—if you will allow me to advise you."

"I allow, and I agree," Khana said, thinking that there should be no thread left to tie them to the dead past, and that the sooner those last remaining threads were severed, the sooner they would be. . .free.

He looked at Joolia.

"*Can* it be now?" he asked.

She smiled. "Sure can. There's an Admin Portal right at the Green Line Mall."

Khana blinked, trying to recall the station map.

Joolia's smile became a grin. She stepped forward, and tucked one hand around his arm, and the other around Bar Jan's good arm.

"I'll show you," she said. "Might as well get it done."

#

Green Line Mall was a shopping area, up two levels from the ARTS halls. While Bar Jan and Joolia were inside, filing the necessary forms, Khana went for a walk around the mall.

Despite it being well into alt-shift, there were people about, shopping, eating, walking together. No one seemed panicked, or, indeed, worried, and he supposed that the news of the upcoming comet strike had not yet been shared by Port Admin.

Well, and nor had Khana shared the news with Bar Jan, though it would have been difficult to stem the enthusiastic flow of his conversation.

For it would seem that Bar—no. It would seem that *Jeef* had found a new course for himself. He had entertained them with tales of the kitchens behind the Cantina, and the wonders of baking bread. Chef Klyken had invited Jeef to come and observe at his own restaurant, once he was no longer a medical dependent of the Port. That, Khana thought, was promising. If Jeef's interest was constant, perhaps he would earn a position in this Klyken's kitchen, while Khana...

While Khana what? he asked himself, half-amused. He, who had planned for them both for so long, had not planned for himself beyond a certain yearning to be of use. He would of course place himself on the volunteer roster, but he had yet to consider anything long-term. For half his lifetime, he had cared for the heir of Rinork, and he had assumed that the tale of his life would hold very little change, save that which occurred when the heir ascended to delm.

But now, his life was upended, and it would seem that his charge, neither heir nor delm, would not for much longer require, or, indeed, want his care.

It was an odd thought—that all his care might be for. . .himself.

Whatever, he thought with sudden wryness, he might choose to call himself.

He finished his arc through the shops, and was strolling back to the Admin Portal, when the door opened, and. . .Jeef came out. He was smiling broadly, like a Terran, and there was an ID card in his good hand.

Behind him came Joolia, looking tired, but also smiling.

Khana stretched his legs to meet them.

"All's well?" he asked.

"Well and more than well!" Jeef declared, holding up the card so Khana could read that it was coded to Jeef Baker.

"Baker?" Khana asked.

"Joolia tells me that it is a well-used Terran name. As it is also the profession I hope to follow, it seemed. . .a good choice."

"A good choice, indeed," Khana said, producing his own smile.

"Your turn," Joolia said.

He looked up to meet her eyes; nodded.

"Jeef—"

"Go, I will be well," Jeef said, using his chin to point to the public screen. "When you are done, find me reading the news."

#

"Here," Joolia said, pointing at the screen. "This is where you input your name. It's got be no less than two words and no more than five. OK?"

"Yes," he breathed, and stared at the place where he was to put his. . .name. Khana vo'Daran Clan Baling was dead by his own will, so Rinork would inform Baling. The life-price would likely already have been paid, Rinork being meticulous in such things. While it was unlikely that Baling would set a bounty on him, Rinork assuredly would, on Bar Jan. For Rinork's purpose, Khana was nothing other than a loose thread to be cut.

"If you're not ready," Joolia said, softly. "We can come back later."

"Sooner is better," he said, and looked down to the input pad.

In the space labeled *Call-name* he placed *Shanna.* It was a thread that tied him, past to present, honoring the choices he had made. He looked at it on the screen—Shanna. Yes. It was correct.

"One more," Joolia said next to his ear. "The Port has a list you can pick from, if you don't have something particular in mind."

"Yes, please," he said.

She reached past him to tap the screen, and a list unfurled down the right side.

He scrolled, frowning—and used his finger to arrest the scroll.

"Newman," he said. "That is apt."

"Then make it your own," Joolia said, and he placed the name in the appropriate space.

"All right, now there's some questions," Joolia said. "Won't take long."

#

They exited the Portal and found Jeef sitting on a bench across from the door. He was not smiling.

Shanna went forward.

"What has happened?" he asked.

Jeef jerked his head, and it was then that Shanna saw that there was a crowd around the public screen. A silent and strangely tense crowd.

"The comet," Jeef said. "No, I mistake. A piece of the comet. It will strike the station. So." He looked back to Shanna, and it seemed he tried to smile.

"There is something said in Terran," he said then. "About living joy, no matter how short a time?"

"A short life," Joolia said, "but a merry one."

"Yes," said Jeef, "that is it."

"The Port has shields," Joolia said, extending a hand to help him to his feet. "It's survived strikes before. There are several reports in the library. I wouldn't figure this comet's going to win, just yet."

Shanna felt the muscles of his stomach loosen, even as he offered his arm to Joolia.

"What, then, should we do?"

"Honestly? We should go back home and get some rest before day shift catches us asleep on our feet."

THREE

They were woken by a bell, loud and unaccustomed, followed by Ferlandy's voice over the little-used intercom.

"Special Session for ARTS in an hour," he said. "Attendance mandatory."

#

Shanna and Jeef broke their fast with cheese muffins and tea, and arrived at the lounge to find it already awash in ARTS residents. They took two chairs together at the end of a row near the front, settling just as Ferlandy strode in and took his place behind the front table.

"We're having a guest today, so no sharing," he said briskly. "She should be—"

He paused, and Shanna heard the brisk step in the hallway. Heads turned as the tall woman in a Port Admin uniform strode into the room. There was a sudden uproar, as some residents clapped hands, others whistled, and many came to their feet.

"Residents and Travelers, I see most of you know our guest already," Ferlandy said, his voice raised over the racket, "so I'll just step back and let Chief Operator Malvern have the floor for as long as she needs it."

Malvern came to the front table and paused, looking at them, as they looked at her. There was, Shanna thought, a fell energy to her that had never been apparent when they had met at the Cantina. This woman was a delm, a commander, practical and hard.

"So." She greeted them all with a single nod, and began to speak.

"Some of you might not've heard that the Port's attempt to nudge the incoming comet away from us by directing the mining equipment trapped on the surface to move wasn't our most notable success. The comet broke apart, and while two big pieces are gonna give us some room, the third's likely gonna hit. That's better than the whole thing hits us, but it's still not good.

"You also might not've heard that Chas Debiro and his entire shift of Port Controllers left on the Veddy Line's big freighter a couple days ago. His back-up left with most of her shift next ship out, same day—that was *Ozwall*, which had filed for quick departure.

"Seems the upgraded shielding and brand-new comet capturing protocol you'll remember we had done couple Standards back, that project headed by Chief Debiro, isn't so robust as the contractor and the chief would have had Admin believe."

She paused to look out over the room, but no one spoke, nor moved. It was possible, Shanna thought, remembering to do it himself, that no one breathed.

Malvern nodded.

"Yeah, there's crimes, and malfeasance, and criminal intent, but that's not my problem, nor yours. *Our* problem is keeping Port Chavvy's people safe."

Her mouth moved, a smile, Shanna thought, wry and wistful.

"I retired as Chief Operator nineteen Standards back, but before I did that, I thought of, designed, tested, and put into place the Port Chavvy Structural Emergency Response Protocols. According to that document, in an emergency like we have now, the Port Controllers implement the protocols and procedures. Since we seem to be out of Port Controllers, I got called up from Reserve to sit back down in Ops Seat One, in charge of implementing the protocols and procedures.

"Which brings me to why I'm here, talking to you."

She paused again, but her audience sat rapt.

"Right. Short tell is this: Step three in the protocols, subhead long-term emergency, is *take stock of human potential.* That's everybody on this station, including you, including me."

Windy stood up. "You're counting *us*? What for?"

Malvern smiled at him.

"Good question, and put straight. 'preciate that. What's your name?"

"Wi–Wallace VinHalin, ma'am. Awaitin' Transport."

"Pleased to meet you, Mr. VinHalin. Now the reason I'm *counting you* is that the Station's gotta run, and we need a certain number of people to make sure that all the necessary jobs are covered at least twice. By necessary jobs I mean stinks, and maintenance, food service, engineering, life support, communications—all of it, saving Port Admin because for the duration of the emergency that particular seat belongs to me."

She raised a hand.

"So, before anybody says that we already got triple redundancy on almost all jobs on-station, I'll say, that's *now*, before we evacuate."

She stopped talking then because the word *evacuate* had elicited a response from the group, a sort of a startled murmur, Shanna thought, folding his hands tightly together on his knee.

The murmur having died, Malvern spoke again.

"Yeah, we're evacuating. Kids, olds, med-cases, those'll go first, each with one caregiver. Then we'll move down to those who don't wanna stay in harm's way. Outstation Quince isn't even gonna see the comet go past, so we're putting as many as we can under the dome. Ships in port can take the overflow. Planetary Admin is talking about sending shuttles up, taking anybody who don't mind dirt downside. We could get everybody out, and would, if the situation was more dangerous than what we got."

She paused, as if struck by what she had just said, then smiled slightly and shook her head.

"What we got is dangerous enough for me. But there'll still be a station to come home to, even if that rock with our name on it strikes truer than projections. So what I'm looking for is people who will stay, and keep Port Chavvy running, and do whatever needs doing during and after the collision.

"Here's what I can guarantee: things will be confusing; there'll be more work than hands, which is a new kind of problem; and it'll be dangerous. We're looking at dealing with anything from a major breach—in which case people will die—to watching a couple antennas get ripped out of our array.

There came a rumble of voices. Malvern continued to talk, louder, asserting her precedence.

"The other things I can guarantee: Everybody who stays and helps keep Port Chavvy up and running, will get three meals a day, bunk space, training as necessary, and, when the emergency is over and Admin takes back its damn chair—all the emergency volunteers will be recognized as having fulfilled their residency requirements."

Silence overflowed the lounge, as if those present utterly disbelieved what they had just heard. Shanna felt his blood quicken. Residency! He could do more than volunteer, he could learn a trade, he could—

"In just a few minutes, I'll ask those who are volunteering to come up here and talk to Mr. Ferlandy. There's some questions to be answered, and so forth. Before we do that, though, we need to get the med-cases on their way to safety. There are two, I think, Mr. Ferlandy?"

"Yes'm. Cazzy's still under clinic-care, but—" He glanced out over the lounge.

Shanna felt a movement in the seat beside him, as Jeef rose to his full meager height, the empty sleeve of his lab coat pinned neatly out of the way.

"Jeef Baker," he said. "I volunteer to stay and work for the safety of the Port."

Malvern frowned at him.

"Medics let you go?" she asked.

"They have not yet. Will there be no medics among those who remain?"

The frown eased.

"We'll have medics. Tell me what you can do for me, Jeef Baker."

He inclined his head, very Liaden in that gesture.

"I can read. I can do inventory. I can cipher. I can—"

"Follow orders?" Malvern interrupted.

Jeef took a breath, and this time inclined from the waist.

"Yes," he said.

"Then get yourself up to the clinic, right now. Tell 'em I sent you for a work eval. Tell 'em you volunteered for Comet Utility Crew. You bring whatever the medics give you back to Mr. Ferlandy, here. Got that?"

"Yes," Jeef said again. He stepped out of the row, walking out of the lounge without a backward glance.

Shanna thought about going after him, took a breath and remained seated.

When he looked up, Malvern gave him a nod and a smile.

#

They were issued Port volunteer vests, protective gloves, goggles, and a utility belt. Every sixth of them, by count-off, was issued a comm unit, and that person became a team leader. As a group, they were known as *Uties,* and their first duty was to assist in the evacuation, keeping order among those moving to the docks and the ships that would take them to safety. As each apt was cleared, it was entered by a Utie, who verified that no one had been left behind before using their Admin-issued general key to trigger the inflation of air bags that would keep furniture in place, should—when—the comet struck the station.

As Uties were rotated out of escort-and-lockdown, they were given tours of vents, stink-pots, utility cabinets, wiring and plumbing closets, tool-bins, and emergency hatches.

The tool-bin proved unexpectedly exhilarating for Shanna, as the tools within were handed around and named as a primer to their duties.

"Bash bar," said their tutor, handing it to the first of the group, who obediently repeated the phrase and passed it to the Utie on her right.

"Life-pry," the tutor continued, "stinks hammer, starbar. . ."

Shanna flinched as that came to hand, sagging with the weight of it. He had not seen the instrument of his master's maiming, and had imagined something. . .powered and smooth. But this object was evidently meant to be used violently, and was clearly capable of damaging the fabric of Port Chavvy itself, much less the fabric of a Liaden lordling's expensive port-side coat sleeve, and the arm it embraced.

Jeef, separated from him by several of their team members, his wounded arm now enclosed in a flexible cast that allowed him to fully occupy his shirt and vest, received the starbar in his good hand, and went to one knee, bearing the weight of the thing to the deck.

"Yeah, starbar'll getcher attention, all right!" said the Utie on his right, reaching down and hefting the thing as if it were a twig.

Jeef regained his feet, caught Shanna's worried eye and bowed with subtle irony.

#

The evacuees departed; the Uties' work shifts grew longer and more frantic. The images of the onrushing comet were on all the news screens, the constant beauty of them dimmed by the other information that they absorbed as they worked: the protoplanet had been being mined for metals and ice; and among the metals nickel and iron were common, with a smattering of the heavier elements. Shanna found Jeef's interest in the technical side of things imposing but not surprising; he seemed more at home among real things than the fripperies of etiquette and dominance that had been so commonplace in their *melant'i*-ridden past.

Word came that the station's maneuvering jets and pocket engine were useless in the present emergency. Port Chavvy could, indeed, be relocated, but not quickly enough to avoid its oncoming doom. The question of tugs pulling the station out of the way was dismissed by the engineers as likely to cause more structural damage than the comet's kiss.

The Uties worked on.

Most of the store fronts of the various malls and shopping districts were no longer air-tight, despite the maintenance rules requiring it. Rumors went through the decks that certain owners had paid bribes to be excused from higher levels of compliance, with Malvern promising damnation and worse to anyone she might prove it against. The Uties condensed the goods in the stores around the known pipes, conduits, and air vents in an attempt to allay the potential damage from objects traveling at the rate of a kilometer or more a second.

And then the comet broke again, becoming ash and dense cores, spinning madly.

Aghast, an on-break team stood watching the streaming, nearly foaming mass of hurtling objects split away from the larger masses in a view from a probe. Some parts appeared to adhere to the pockmarked centers, others spewed away as if under power. Portions, at least, were still on course for the station.

"But why?" Shanna asked while shaking his head, "Why this chaos now, why like this?"

He'd expected no answer, but Jeef's quiet voice came, as if trying to soothe with explanation.

"Transition phases, Shanna, change of state. The coma—the comet-head—is not an atmosphere, has almost no pressure whatsoever and with the approach to the inner system the ices become gas without being liquid—they boil. Then in the starlight they look like they burn into smoke or turn to ribbons, but there's no flame. Just a change of state."

Around them a mix of nodding and shaking heads, and an echo, "Just a change of state, that's all."

#

Malvern had ordered everyone who remained into the core safe lounges, where they strapped in, fresh batteries in their comms, food and water packs to hand, with pressure masks and breathers. They had done everything they could, all they had been asked to do, and more. Now, they waited for the impact. Any other duty lay on the far side of that event.

The all-station intercom snapped, and here came Malvern's voice.

"Strapped in and waiting," she said. "You got what I got. There's maybe a chance these things are gonna rush by and we won't have to worry about 'em til we hit this section of the orbit again in five Standards. But that's a *maybe* chance, and I don't think we're gonna get that lucky. So, stay strapped in, be ready to call your leaders. *Zanzo's Flitter* is standing off, observing. They sent a radar image of a mess of stuff—the rocks and what they've attracted—coming through our intersection in fifty-eight minutes. There may be rapid accelerations. Strap down. Stay strapped down until I send all clear!"

#

Scarcely ten minutes had elapsed when the comm blared again.

"Movement in the Long View! Chef Klyken, acknowledge!"

There was a pause, then again, more urgently. "Long View, acknowledge!"

There was a grunt in his ear, and Jeef was up, unstrapped, in danger.

"Stay!" Shanna cried. "What are you—"

"Klyken," Jeef snapped. "I will get him!"

And he was gone, running.

Shanna repeated several of the useful new words he had learned as a Utie, released his own webbing, and ran after.

#

The window—it was the window that gave the Long View Restaurant its name. Jeef remembered that it was said to be tougher than hull-plate. He remembered the view, the long swell of stars, against the black of space.

Now, the window opened on mud and dust. Objects struck it, audibly.

And Klyken was nowhere to be seen.

Jeef turned on his heel, straining to see in the meager light of the emergency dims.

"Klyken?" he called.

There was no answer.

No, Jeef thought suddenly. Klyken would not be *here* where other people ate what he had made for them.

Klyken would be in the kitchen.

He spun and bolted through the pass-door.

The kitchen was locked down, pristine, and empty.

The door worked at his back, and Shanna was there. He spun.

"Go!"

"Come with me! Jeef, this is too dangerous!"

"Yes!" he shouted. "It is dangerous! Shanna—go! You already died of me once! I will find Chef Klyken—he must be here!"

"Perhaps he is tied down," Shanna suggested, not leaving.

"Here?" Jeef said, with a shudder, imagining the damage. "Malvern wants everyone in the core lounges. Shanna—"

"Yes, I will go. Let us find the chef, first."

There was no more time to argue, if they were, indeed, to find Klyken and bring them all safely to the core.

Jeef moved down the aisle, came to the freezer, the bread safe, the—

The bread safe.

He put his hand on the latch, but it was locked.

"Klyken?" he called.

There was no answer.

"Jeef, he is not here, or he does not want to be rescued." Shanna came down the other aisle. "Come, we must save ourselves."

"Go," he said. "I—" He bit his lip, as memory rose.

It isn't a good thing, to throw a child away. The Long View—that is my child now.

He took a breath. It was dishonest, what he was about to do, and the book made a strong case for honesty in all things, even as it also instructed one to care for those in need.

Surely, Jeef thought, here is need.

"Father!" he called, sharply. "Father, I am here!"

For a long moment, nothing happened. The clicking against the window was loud in the silence. Shanna extended a hand.

The latch of the bread safe moved. Klyken stepped out, holding a stasis box.

He paused on the threshold of the room, and Jeef had a momentary fear that he would bolt back inside.

Then, the chef nodded.

"Yes," he said, quietly. "I had only wanted my bread-heart."

FOUR

The largest rock destroyed much of the comm and power array in a single jolting strike that took an hour of Malvern's superb piloting of station resources to quell.

The ashen remains of the smaller rock smashed into dust on the Long View's window.

The middle-sized rock passed through the shattered remains of Port Chavvy's array, flew by the dusty detritus splattered by the small rock, and left no additional trace to add to the confusion already spawned.

#

The last of the evacuees was home, joining forces with the Uties, as they repaired the damage the comet, and neglect, had done.

The station had paid each Utie a "stake," and issued each a new card, declaring them to be Residents of Port Chavvy Station. They still lived in the ARTS halls, as apts were being repaired and made ready for them.

Shanna was now full-time leader of a Utie team. He'd kept the toolset he'd been assigned for the duration of the emergency in their rooms for eleven days, for quick response in case one more lump of the comet managed to find the Port, but it hadn't happened and both he and Jeef were relieved once the set that included starbars and stinks hammers went back to their emergency closets rather than bulking large just inside their own door. Jeef was Klyken's apprentice, certified and formal, and most of his hours were spent in the Long View, repairing and cleaning with the rest of Klyken's workers—and also learning somewhat of baking.

At the Admin level, investigations were underway, and a team of auditors had come up from the planet to assist.

Shanna was crossing the lounge, thinking of a shower before he joined the usual group to go in search of supper. This was a better habit than backstairs at the delm's residence, with none of the tension of those rule-bound precincts. Joolia and he had taken to walking apart from the group after the meal was done, going up to the Atrium on E Deck, which had taken only a little damage from the comet.

"Shanna!" a voice came, sharp and unexpected from the right. He stopped, and turned to face Femta; a talkative Femta, as it happened.

"Just the man I wanted to see! A friend of mine got in today, first time on port. I wonder if you'd be willing to meet him and me at the Atrium on E Deck, at purple. There's a couple others coming, too. We've got an offer to put in front of you."

Shanna frowned slightly.

"A job?"

"A job?" Femta nodded. "You could call it that, sure."

Uties did worthy work, but Shanna had lately been thinking about what he might prefer to do, as his service to the port and to people.

"I would be interested," he said, and Femta grinned.

"Good, then. See you at purple."

#

He let the dinner group get ahead of him, and realized that he was not alone.

"Going up to the garden again?" Joolia asked.

"Yes, but tonight I am to meet Femta and his friend, to hear about a job."

Joolia grinned.

"Funny thing—me, too."

Shanna tipped his head, not liking to think of Joolia as. . .competition. However—

"I figure it can't hurt to listen to what they got to say," Joolia continued. "Might be inneresting; might not."

"Yes," he said, and offered his arm. "Let us go together."

"Great idea," she said, and slipped her arm through his.

#

It had just come purple when they strolled into the Atrium, to find Femta and another person awaiting them at the first grouping of benches.

"Just on time," Femta said, and urged his companion forward. "This is my colleague of many years, Jemmon Fairkin, who has come to fetch me away! Jemmon, this is Joolia Tenuta and Shanna Newman."

The man was bulky and bald. A long fine silver chain depended from his left ear. He bowed in the Terran style, one hand over his heart, the other held loose at his side.

"Joolia Tenuta, Shanna Newman, I am happy to see you."

"We invited one more to speak with us this evening. He did warn that he might be a little behind the—"

There came the sharp sound of bootheels on decking, and 'round the curve of the path came a figure dressed in white, carrying a tray in two hands.

"Here I am," Jeef said, "late as promised! I bring my first batch of *cupcakes*, to balance my tardiness."

He came up with them, and smiled, a scent of citrus and sugar wafting in with him.

"Joolia. Shanna. Good evening."

"Good evening," Joolia said, adding, "cupcakes?"

"Do not expect very much," Jeef said, stepping forward to place the tray on one of the benches. "I am told that they are misshapen and mis-decorated, which is true, and my fault for jostling them too much for curiosity while baking. But they taste very good, if I say it myself."

"Then I'll close my eyes when I eat one," Joolia said solemnly and Jeef smiled.

"A perfect solution."

Each chose a sweet and a seat, and for a few minutes there was silence, while they gave the food its due. Jeef had not misrepresented his efforts. The little cakes were very lopsided and the icing unevenly spread, faults that did not detract at all from the pleasing taste.

"Very good!" Joolia pronounced. "Thank you."

"You are welcome," Jeef said.

Femta shifted subtly on the bench, and all attention was immediately on him.

"Now, Jemmon needs to be brought up to the present, so I'll just tell him real quick that all three of you earned Port Chavvy Resident status during the recent comet emergency. These folks have the right to call Port Chavvy their home, to use it as a home port, and receive care and food, if needed. They've gotten a bonus for their work during the emergency—and they'll receive the Resident Basic Allotment, plus whatever they earn by working for the Port. All clear?"

"Clear," Jemmon said with a nod.

"Right." Femta turned to them. "Now, I'll ask you—what do you intend to do with the rest of your lives? You're secure here. Will you stay on and be busy for the Port?

"Will you look up legal references, and mine the archives for Admin for the rest of your life, Joolia? Do you think it will take that long to wind up affairs against the runaways?

"What will you do, Jeef, with your background in trade—be a buyer for a shop on a rebuilt C deck?

"And you, Shanna, you have experience running a household and in dealing with fashion and grooming needs for another. Both of you have impeccable Liaden form and language and both of you will find it hard to make use of your knowledge of Liaden culture here, where *Wynhael* is a rare visitor at best."

A pause as Femta looked hard at each of them, and then to his colleague, who nodded agreement with the questions.

"We have no interest in *Wynhael*," Jeef said quietly. "And she has no interest in us. I hope you have not built plans on the profit you hope to gain by selling us back to her, friend Femta, for you will go broke."

Femta raised both hands, fingers spread. "Nothing like that, friend Jeef. Will you let me follow my questions with my offer?"

Jeef nodded.

"I feel that the three of you have more scope than Port Chavvy. Consider what your lives will be, if you remain in a world encompassed by seven levels. Walking the same halls, waiting for the same ships to come back, on the same schedules, and of course the construction, interruption, and inconveniences of the repair and rebuild. It would be, understand, a good life—or not a bad one. Security is a powerful draw.

"What we offer—Jemmon and me—is an option that is less secure, that has the potential to help thinking people, and to demonstrate to the numberless cultures across space that we are the same more than we are different.

"What we suggest, is that you join us, to help us explore, and learn, and share what we've learned. We will accomplish our goal by—traveling. Being travelers. We will take ship, arrive, explore places—planets, stations, ships—using what we know to entertain ourselves and enlighten others, learning from them the things—food, music and songs—the customs that are unique and the customs that beneath things echo other places."

"What's your funding?" Joolia asked. "Who's your sponsor? I like the notion of traveling, but I don't want to be stranded. Never again."

Jemmon nodded this time, and cleared his throat.

"Femta and I hold tenured university positions as traveling professors of civil culture. We are funded by a revolving grant from Crystal Energy Systems. Among the things we do is study business practices, cultures, custom. We give presentations and reports to librarians, universities, teaching colleagues. Our methods are varied. We can stand in a bar and trade stories with the locals, if that is what we wish to do. What we must not do—is argue the superiority of one culture over another. What we must understand—and by experiencing things first hand we *shall* understand!—is how best to let the worlds of thinking people behave well toward each other.

"We have funding for the first five Standards of travel, which will be distributed among the first of us, whether that be two or five. We expect in seven years to be joined by two more colleagues and have the option of adding one or two along the way, should we find like minds. We shall be a happy tour group, learning, enjoying, witnessing. . .and if we can make worlds work better by quietly insinuating information, by pointing to successes without demanding they be followed, by locating people who are mis-cultured and ought to be elsewhere, as you may have been, Jeef. . ."

Jemmon leaned back, and exchanged a look with Femta.

"So. In three days, Jemmon and I will depart Port Chavvy with tickets to three planets over the next two Standards in hand. We ask you to join us, that we be useful to the universe. You don't have to decide now, but—soon."

"This offer, this opportunity now? This would be a major change of state, I think," said Jeef, glancing to Shanna and back to Femta.

Shanna nodded, allowing himself to wonderingly exhale.

"Change of state, indeed," he murmured.

Shanna was aware that he was shivering. To visit a planet again? To be of use? To travel under his own direction, and for himself? His nodding had never stopped, and he smiled.

"Yes," he said, his voice mingling with Joolia's, "Yes!"

Jeef shook his head, a Terran habit he'd grown to admire. His face was thoughtful, perhaps wistful.

"No."

He paused, looked into the faces of his friends.

"Shanna, Joolia. I have a place here, and the smallness of the world I live in pleases me. I have chosen a trade, and I will learn to be something other than I was. Jeef Baker is the man I wish to be!"

He smiled at Shanna.

"And I will be pleased to see you, brother, when you come home again."

Command Decision

Steve Miller

"Daltrey's still waiting in holding orbit. Wants to know why we haven't solved this yet! If the CMEs clear up he figures they can be down in thirty hours or so."

The intel officer, Lizardi, spoke low, just in case someone had a mic working nearby. She and her companion leaned against a rail fence at the top of steep slope, observing.

Bjarni, the ad hoc planetary specialist—by dint of being the only member of the unit to have been on world before—nodded.

"I had a note, too. Says Righteous Bispham's making noises re contract specs. Daltrey still wants to be there to turn the Nameless over to the Bispham, and the Bispham wants to Name them before they act. Silly damn. . ."

"Local custom," she said, with more than a little asperity.

After a pause, "You know, I think Daltrey's hoping to get out. If he gave me terms I'd buy him out. I think we could keep it together just fine."

The specialist nodded. Everyone always says they want a chance to be the boss.

"Any luck?" she asked after a moment of silence.

Bjarni took a deep breath, recalled his mission. His sensitive nose tried, but disappointed.

The planet smelled green when it didn't stink of sulfur from the open wounds of the tectonics. The seacoasts and islands smelled green with the giant seasonal rafts of seaweed spicing the tricky winds, the brief plains had smelled green with the waves of grasses. . .and now the mountains smelled green of the great bristling tar-spotted pine analogues and the moss-walled rocks of the upswept basalt.

Years since he'd first smelled it as a traveling student. This time—he'd had a sunny tour so far instead of a war, landing ships aground and mired in swamp after taking damage from the stellar storms that had grounded both sides as far as the mercenary units went. They'd managed to get their hovercraft out of the landing ship, but were on the wrong side of the mountain when those comms went haywire and some of them crisped, grounding them the second time.

Elsewhere around the planet the green scent might be over-ridden with the scent of blood, of burning fields, of weapons cobbled out of machines meant for peace, the ozone of overworked electronics and overlay. This mountain had none of those, being as comfortably rural as a rustic guided tour.

The scent he really sought, the one that had intoxicated him on his private visit to InAJam as a youthful wandering philosophy student, was the cusp of green fungi. He'd been entranced by InAJam; he had some of the language and loved it, and more, he loved the food and admired the people. He even dreamed about the place. The most frequent dream was about the ripple he'd seen, when the fragrance of the carpet growths intensified and the colors changed as the spores of one generation fell on the neighboring growths from another, changing them.

"I smell something," Major Lizardi said, but her nose still had a hard time separating the wood flavoring from the aroma of over-cooked meat, as he'd seen at dinner the night before. She blamed that on growing up on Surebleak, and if she survived long enough she'd eventually get a taste for finer things, but she'd likely not be able to smell a ripple in action.

He pointed then to the small sand pile and said, "Cat!"

She wrinkled her nose then, and said, "Not that!"

Bjarni's nose tried again, and he turned to his companion, shaking his head Terran-style, adding the laconic, "No," emphasized with a sigh, "not that either. Not from this direction, anyway."

"They're out there somewhere! They can't let this ripple go unnamed!"

She, of course, had never seen a ripple and while his experience was slight, hers was from training vid and poorly prepared sleep learning. On the other hand she was right—the New Decade was to be declared within the next three days, and the local beliefs required any ripple coinciding with a new year to be celebrated and named and feted.

The politics of that new decade had brought the mercs into play; but who expected the centerpiece of the event to be stolen away so that the planet might be without their most important export for years? He grimaced thinking of the loss to the gastronomes of the galaxy if the untouched initiates didn't come together somewhere by the appointed time.

One of the things Daltrey did right was letting the officers chance the food—their local cooks fed him very well and the others enough. While Lizardi tried the fungi she wasn't a fan, like he was. He'd tried to introduce some of the others, explaining that they were not in fact eating cat, as numerous as *they* were around, but a variation of shroom with touches of this and that protein and. . .and it wasn't proper meat from hoof or vat, and they grumped about it, going with bar rations and instant soups. Bjarni reveled in all of InAJam, especially the food.

Which was why Bjarni was out beyond the lines on an alien mountainside with the intel officer, sniffing the winds of morning, hoping to sense a sign of the missing religionists or their rogue captors. That was what *she* was searching for. Something to tell Daltrey, some hint of how they'd win this thing, after all.

They stared down the green sides awhile longer on this, the sacred side of the hill, looking toward the most distant and all but invisible sea, before turning toward the awkward pod camp in the lee of their downed hovercraft beside the idyllic lake.

#

The other side of the mountain felt crowded. Soldiers guarded busily, as if they were able to do something real while waiting to be rescued, a rescue depending on one side or the other winning so that they might be either ransomed or lifted from this place by a working ship. Too, there were pilgrims, wandering through, offering food and oddities on their way up the mountain.

Bjarni smiled at a couple trying to sell him a carved bird, touching hand to forehead and speaking the local language and telling them, "I have too many already. How would I feed more?"

They laughed, touched hands to forehead in response, a real smile coming back.

"The locals act like they know you," Lizardi said before they parted. "Are these regulars?"

Shake of the head. "They may be—there are a few I've seen before—but I think there's a special smile, almost a family expression, you get after you've sat at meals here, when you speak the language."

She shrugged, "Might be it. It feel like they all recognize you."

He shrugged back—"I feel at home here, Major. I guess it shows."

The continent they were on was basically flat, with three folds of hills that rose to these mountains, the central high point of the continent where most of the people loved the flat lands.

Here, the lake, on a high plateau with one last taller hill swathed in vines and berry brambles behind it, overlooking their camp site. That last hill also held a religious refuge, a temple occupied by a few fanatics who could sometimes be seen standing, watching the plants grow, else soothing them with water and fish-meal. Pilgrims came and went, bringing food for the most pious and taking away whatever they might learn on the hillside.

The pilgrims were also anticipating the High Ripple—something that came once every fifty standards or so, and which coincided this time with the Decade. The signs had been good that this was the year the six variants would all prove good to spore and mix.

Below their plateau, which was occupied by the few ground-side forces of Daltrey's Daggers—was another reached by a barely tended road, home of a small town. From that town was a spiderweb of paths and rough roads leading in all directions, and below that were a series of hills and lakes leading to a plain. The daily pilgrims came that way, past the soldiers, and up into the sacred.

What exactly the sacred was for the locals Bjarni wasn't sure. To him it was the whole of the planet—a single month roaming about as a student on memtrek between course years had convinced him that he wanted to retire here. The war so far hadn't unconvinced him.

He'd written papers about his student experience. He'd mentioned the ripple, standing on a deck and watching the ground cover slowly go from one shade of green to another over a few hours as seasons changed, as the dominant fungi's spores spread themselves into the mat of greenery underlying all. When his home ship's fortunes waned and it was auctioned away from the family—they really should have listened to him!—he'd ended up destitute rather than a student, stuck on the other side of the galaxy, saved by a merc recruiter's happy offer of employment.

To this day, a dozen years plus on active duty and another three between calls, he thought of himself as exactly what he was—an administrator par excellence, a logistical technician making the force able to fight when it wanted to, with records impeccable and practical to keep everything in order, who happened to work as a merc. Intel Major Lizardi had ferreted out his InAJam connections and brought him on board for this tour.

In his pod Bjarni went over the latest news, of which there wasn't much–The mercs on either side hadn't got permission to put the action on hold while the fighting infrastructure got put back together. Instead Daltrey's orbital office sent multiple instances of the same command with the hopes that someone would pay attention and the Bandoliers did the same for their side. Neither side knew the whereabouts of a certain important group of people and neither side wanted to give too much information the other side could use. No one even knew what they looked like!

"The young people" was the phrase that kept being used, The Nameless!

Bjarni'd watched the wording of communiques, watched what weather reports they could get, and handled the ongoing inventorying and replenishment lists—not much else to do!—and waited for dinner. He wasn't sorry when he left his databases for the day, trudging down to dinner in the makeshift mess hall with the late dusk skies already colored with the twisty bands of reds and yellows, purples and greens, as the auroras flared anew—or judging by the comm techs, continued to flare. He'd picked up a small parade of cats along the way, as he so often did here, and they walked him delicately to the mess hall, and were still there in the full dark to walk him back to his pod under the intricate flowing colors of the night.

#

He hadn't let any cats in, but something woke him from his vague dream of shrouded faces, piercing eyes, and the sounds of local rhythms. A sound? An aroma?

Bjarni sniffed, catching nothing but ordinary scents, but he knew he'd sensed something! The dream? Could he have been smelling this in his sleep? Could something have leaked in from outdoors?

He walked to the door, glanced into the night to see the aurora, muted to slight shimmers.

He sniffed once, hard.

No joy. No joy. He'd know, that he was sure. He'd smell when the ripple came through, know that the initiates had done the deed and melded the newest food, or failed. He'd also recall those eyes!

#

In the late afternoon next day Bjarni broke from his logistical and admin duties, and walked away from the busyness of camp, unsurprised to find the sharp-faced Lizardi out as well, standing by her pod as if waiting for him. The planet felt good to be on, even if there was war and destruction elsewhere, and being out in it a necessity turned pleasure.

Bjarni nodded at the major, and she back, and they proceeded wordlessly.

They passed by the guards on the well trodden path leading toward the temple. The rules were clear—they were not to approach the temple without invite—and none from that structure had bothered even to survey the medical camp or its denizens. Other locals had come from the town below, seen that the strangers were settled well, and gone, some to the temple and some back down, in what was a constant stream of locals.

It had taken the guards awhile to get used to the prohibition on detaining all the pilgrims who wandered through camp: it was a given that someone dressed for pilgrimage was indeed a pilgrim. It was written: pilgrims do not engage in warfare.

The compromise Daltrey had reached with his counterparts in the local forces and the other side was that people—the pilgrims themselves—need not be searched. Could not be searched.

The baskets and packs they had might be searched, but not individuals; and for that matter standing orders said no shooting of wildlife, and especially no shooting, eating, or killing of cats. The cat thing didn't bother him, and the good behavior of the unarmed pilgrims made them as much curiosity as problem.

It was a confused war, far from Daltrey's Daggers' finest hour. They'd signed on to help defend one side's Decadal Ritual from interruption only to discover that this wasn't a simple binary argument but a long-brewing fight among a dozen different groups, most showing changeable allegiance. And that Decadal Ritual? If it was a failure, there'd be crop shortages or worse, and the rulers got to find new jobs—or new heads.

This time, instead of looking down, they looked up. There were birdish creatures hovering and swooping, among which a dozen drones might have hidden had not rules demanded that no such be flown. The temple was a stark white structure with red lines painted seemingly at random across walls; in the lowering afternoon light it was quite beautiful.

A bustle behind them then, steps nearby. Bjarni felt a twinge in one nostril. Fine spice, fine 'shroom somewhere close.

Alert now, Bjarni twisted where he stood. He recognized the sounds and the style of a walking caravan, people from the flatlands. This particular caravan was swathed each in voluminous robes quilted from the robes of ancestors which had been quilted from robes of ancestors which had been quilted before them.

They carried baskets, all sixteen of them, and they were roped together as proper pilgrims were, basket to basket as one line and person to person as another, walking—here at least—with a low chant. Cats walked with them purposefully, staying close, it appeared, to particular pilgrims, and careful not to impede the march.

Along with the chant there came another twinge. His nostrils flared, and then he realized the it was probably the aromas of the pilgrims' breakfasts or lunch. The song got louder as he moved in their direction—not because he was closer but as if they were gaining in volume as they closed in on their temple above.

Bjarni finally heard some of the words, which were a hymn to the sky with its star that brought the rain. Of course it did—such things were as basic as the aggregation of mass into hydrogen and into star, thence gravity leading to spheres collecting hydrogen and thus to atmosphere, atmosphere and solar energies to weather, weather, gravity, and energy leading to life.

As the pilgrims closed on the pair the steady up-slope breeze broke, so now a dozen scents mingled, all of food worthy of the gods. The locals, poor by galactic standards, ate as well as fatcats and potentates elsewhere. It was an easy world to live on, epicurean food literally underfoot much of the year. This caravan carried a fortune in fragile food.

The leader was a woman of middle years, as tall as he or the intel officer, carrying a basket. Bjarni had seen her the day before, and he thought, days before that as they skirted the enclave, she often the last of them, stopping from time to time to sweep the trail this way or that, or attend to a branch needing repair from their passing. In a real war zone you'd have thought she was looking for sensors!

Today the woman was in front and she eyed Bjarni with care. He had the visible weapon, after all, even if he didn't offer the same demeanor as the camp guards. The middle of the line of travel drew his attention. They moved at a different gait and rhythm—their own and not the leader's, despite the pilgrim ties. Their baskets were smaller than the other travelers.

Also, the air was full now of the scent of 'shroom, from somewhere, the breeze muddling the source.

Bjarni stood as if rooted, watching, caught a glance from that group—

"Inspect!"

Surprised, he looked to Lizardi, who had a palm up indicating the group should stop.

"Spotted something?"

"Not me," she said, "but you're all aquiver!"

"Inspect, now!" This time she raised her voice, placing herself in front of them with both hands raised for emphasis.

Her peremptory demand acknowledged, came a ritual lining up of the group; one by one men and women alike, opened their hand woven baskets and stood back six paces from the potential contagion of the foreigners. The cats however, stayed each and every one behind the baskets they'd walked with, and the chant went on—not by all of the walkers but by a group in the center of the pack—the most devout, perhaps.

The major raised a hand and from the camp came several sentries on a dead run.

Inspection of the locals wasn't usually his job; his job was compliance with an astounding number of rules and regulations. He was in charge of the proper on-time filing of notices, invoices, analyses, and reports as generated by a mercenary unit working on a fringe planet, barely a hundred years this side of being interdicted for Problematic Practices.

In the center of the line, the singers were six youngsters, not farmhands by his guess. They tried to hide in the cowls of their robes as they stood away from their baskets, but they did no good job of it. Still, they kept up their chant, with at least two dozen cats arrayed about them.

Lizardi gestured in their direction and looked at him pointedly as the fluent expert among them. The caravan leader stirred a little, as did several of the others. In an antagonistic population he might have been concerned.

The chant continued. His nose caught nuance of fungi, cooked and uncooked and he felt a rising awareness, almost an arousal as might happen with the very finest of the fungi-concentrates.

He closed with that section of line, and the volume went up again, though they turned somewhat away from him, at least five of them did. The sixth sang something different in the song, something he couldn't quite make out as the hoods muffled words as well as faces.

Walking between the people and their burdens, he saw these baskets each had what he'd now expected, fungi being carried to the mountain. These were not piled high like the other baskets, but were mere handfuls, redolent of the highest quality.

Bjarni mimed throwing hoods back, saying in the dialect—"You may show your faces to the sun, may you not?"

Around him a rush of the cats, flawlessly groomed, crowding him as he was nearly an arms length from the shortest singer. He waded through carefully and—they'd not listened yet.

While the other five singers sang the chant louder, this one sang softer. He looked into the face and saw the eyes of blue-green, his breath catching. He thought, too, that the robed visage was as startled as he. Now he mimed with more force the throwing back of hoods.

As one, they did, revealing beauty. Strong faces, unlined, alert, singing—he was within touching distance now, the song loud, this one with intense eyes singing off-key a little—no, singing special words to him!"

"We knew you would be here, we knew it was you, we knew you would find us, we knew that you could. We are we. . .we grasp the *ĉampinjono*!"

There was a commotion at the end of the line. A sentry stood in front of the leader, not holding her but standing between her and these six. The cats still milled about. . .

The six sang on, loosening further the travel robes, showing exquisite garments beneath.

The singing stopped.

Looking in his face, the beauty in front of him said, "We have the husks, we have a duty. This day should be *the* day, friend, this day should start the ripple!"

"You will do this for us all. You have the touch! I saw your face in a vision, I knew it!"

Bjarni whirled, raised his voice.

"Major, this group. This—force—they walked through our lines in the guise of mere pilgrims. These six must be freed! They must get to the temple now!"

It took her a moment to comprehend the bright colored outfits beneath the robes—and the sentries bore down upon the others with professional interest.

"Mud and blood," she said without heat, seeing those arrayed before her. "Mud and blood times fifty!"

The beautiful one looked into his face and tugged at the ceremonial ropes attaching all together. "These have a magic about them. We cannot fight—if they ran we would have to run with them! We need these bindings taken off!"

Bjarni looked to the major, waved at the initiates. "We must get them to their temple—they tell us it is today. They must have their ritual today!"

He dared to hold the hand of the initiate with the amazing eyes and showed the rope with an extra metallic thread within to Lizardi.

"We have to get this off of them!"

"I don't know the language, Bjarni. You tell them."

Bjarni turned toward the woman who had been leader, now disarmed.

"*Liberigi La Virgulojn*!" he said, repeating it in Trade for all to hear. "Release the virgins!"

#

"Are you coming?"

Lizardi shook her head, waving at the barely controlled confusion about them.

"I can't. I'm going to organize this—" here she laughed—"and then, I have to tell Daltrey he and his friend will have to miss the party. I'm on the spot—command decision and all that."

That quickly he'd been led by the freed virgins and two keepers up the mountainside to the blindingly white buildings where several dozen acolytes cheered their appearance and rushed to preparation. The chant resumed, and grew steadily in volume as passing pilgrims collected to add their voices.

Bjarni was given over-robes to wear, and brought to a thin stone seat, where a pair of attendants appeared, bringing him a bowl of water from a stone pool shimmering in the afternoon light, that he might wash his hands in preparation to witness. . .what?

He sat running over his reading in his head—obviously parts of the rituals were not usually shared with commoners and strangers.

He'd not been expecting the disrobing of initiates, nor the use of the pool as kind of game of ritual cleansing while their bags and cats sat nearby.

The clean and naked virgins leapt from the waters of the sacred pool with no hesitation, charging among the cats to grab handfuls of the colorful fungus from their baskets and then full of excitement rushed to their bower, holding hands and chattering as they flung themselves within.

The coreligionists outside began to sing louder, and two found drums.

Laughter rose from the bower and became passionate, and more such laughter rang out over the mountainside, nearly smothered by the chants.

The drumming and singing went on until there was yet another burst of passion. The shadows on the long lawn lengthened and now the inside of the bower lit up as column after column collected the setting sun's rays and directed them within.

There was singing from within, a shout of cheer. Shortly after the six initiates emerged, one robed in red, one in yellow, one in green, one in blue, one in orange, and the last in purple, each collecting their baskets and the escort of cats.

They came as a group to him, Bjarni, and he stood.

"We, we get to stay here tonight," the one in purple said –"we are not done yet!"

The others laughed in agreement, quick glances stolen among themselves.

"The other part is not done yet, either. We need to collate these *ĉampinjono*, and we wish you, Bjarni, to help. Walk with us."

Walking was not easy—the cats were back, weaving between feet, prancing with tails held high, as if they too were part of the secrets here, they too—here!

They walked to the small apron of green beside the temple—from here they looked down the mountainsides that led to the hills that led to the flat lands, the camp and town behind the temple, unseen.

"Hold your hands together, thus!"

The one in purple made a wide bowl of his hands.

Bjarni followed suit, watching as the youths suppressed smiles, the solemnity growing on every face.

"Hold as that. We shall each place *ĉampinjono* upon your hands. These are not poison!"

Bjarni smiled—yes, many of the mercs had been warned not to eat random plants from this place—but these, these he could smell already!

The virgins—or perhaps the not-virgins—crowded around, discussing in quiet voices, each taking two of the stringy fungi from their baskets and holding them above Bjarni's hands. It was hard for him not snatch one, to bury his face in one, to eat it raw. Overpowering—

"When we drop these in your hands you must squeeze your hands together, squeeze tightly, and hold them. It may be a moment, it may be ten, but warm them but do not look. When they sing you may open your hands and free them. Do you understand?"

He looked from face to face, all beautiful in their own way, all serious, all eager.

He nodded.

That was the moment they rushed to him. Treasure fell into his hands, the *ĉampinjono*, that was the moment he closed his eyes and squeezed. The fungi moved within his hands, as if they lived—but of course they lived! His hands did feel warm and warmer. Sing?

He opened his eyes, seeking direction. The initiates crowded each other, repeating for each other what they'd done for him.

Now his hands felt more movement, and a vibration, heat. From within his grasped hands came a weird sighing and then a clear birdlike sing-song, heard through the chanting still going on. He closed his eyes, sure he could smell the most wonderful scent in the universe—the chirping increased!

Startled, he opened his hands to find not birds but flat rust-golden flakes, vibrating, expanding until they filled his hands to overflowing.

"You may blow them away now, Bjarni. Release The Virgins!"

He did that and saw that each of the initiates was doing the same—opening hands and releasing these. . .

As the flakes hit the carpet of green a great sighing went up. The green turned gold here and there, the spot at his feet and in front of him sighed louder. The rusty gold spread, and hand width, two, three, five, the length of his body. . .the green appearing to flee before it now, the sigh getting louder until the lawn was singing and the colors rushed out into the world, rushing down mountainside at breakneck speed, the world full of the undercurrent of sound, the familiar aroma fascinating, exactly that from his dream.

The six approached then, each rubbing their hands across his, smiling together at the slight gold shimmer of spore-stuff that all seven now shared finger tip to wrist.

There was an awkward moment then, as the initiates looked one from another.

The one with the eyes looked at him, perhaps sternly.

"This ripple is Bjarni's Ripple, now and forever. By morning it will be so around the world. You have freed us to revivify the *ĉampinjono*—and we will remember always the lesson you brought! It will be said for every ripple!"

"Release the Virgins!"

About the Authors

Co-authors Sharon Lee and Steve Miller have been working in the fertile fields of genre fiction for more than thirty years, pioneering today's sub-genre of science fiction romance – stories that contain all the action, adventure and sense of wonder of traditional space opera, with the addition of romantic relationships.

Over the course of their partnership, Lee and Miller have written thirty-one novels, twenty-three in their long-running, original space opera setting, the Liaden Universe®, where honor, wit, and true love are potent weapons against deceit and treachery.

There are more than 300,000 Liaden Universe® novels in print; Liaden titles regularly place in the top ten bestsellers in *Locus Magazine*, the trade paper of the speculative fiction genres; twelve titles have been national bestsellers.

Liaden Universe® novels have twice won the Prism Award for Best Futuristic Romance, reader and editor choice awards from *Romantic Times*, as well as the Hal Clement Award for Best YA Science Fiction Novel, proving the appeal of the series to a wide range of readers.

Lee and Miller's work in the field has not been limited to writing fiction.

Sharon Lee served three years at the first full-time executive director of the Science Fiction and Fantasy Writers of America, and went on to be elected vice-president, and president of that organization. She has been a Nebula Award jurist.

Steve Miller was the founding curator of the University of Maryland's Science Fiction Research Collection. He has been a jurist for the Philip K. Dick Award.

Lee and Miller have together appeared at science fiction conventions around the country, as writer guests of honor and principal speakers. They have been panelists, participated in writing workshops, and given talks on subjects as diverse as proper curating of a cat whisker collection, techniques for creating believable characters, and world-building alien societies.

In 2012, Lee and Miller were jointly awarded the E.E. "Doc" Smith Memorial Award for Imaginative Fiction (aka the "Skylark" Award), given annually by the New England Science Fiction Association to someone who has contributed significantly to science fiction, both through work in the field and by exemplifying the personal qualities which made the late "Doc" Smith well-loved by those who knew him. Previous recipients include George R.R. Martin, Anne McCaffrey, and Sir Terry Pratchett.

Sharon Lee and Steve Miller met in a college writing course in 1978; they married in 1980. In 1988, they moved from their native Maryland to Maine, where they may still be found, in a sun-filled house in a small Central Maine town. Their household currently includes three Maine coon cats.

Steve and Sharon maintain a web presence at korval.com

Novels by Sharon Lee & Steve Miller

The Liaden Universe®: *Agent of Change* * *Conflict of Honors* * *Carpe Diem* * *Plan B* * *Local Custom* * *Scout's Progress* * *I Dare* * *Balance of Trade* * *Crystal Soldier* * *Crystal Dragon* * *Fledgling* * *Saltation* * *Mouse and Dragon* * *Ghost Ship* * *Dragon Ship* * *Necessity's Child* * *Trade Secret* * *Dragon in Exile* * *Alliance of Equals* * *The Gathering Edge* * *Neogenesis* * *Accepting the Lance* * *Trader's Leap*

Omnibus Editions: *The Dragon Variation* * *The Agent Gambit* * *Korval's Game* * *The Crystal Variation*

Story Collections: *A Liaden Universe Constellation: Volume 1* * *A Liaden Universe Constellation: Volume 2* * *A Liaden Universe Constellation: Volume 3* * *A Liaden Universe Constellation: Volume 4*

The Fey Duology: *Duainfey* * *Longeye*

Gem ser'Edreth: *The Tomorrow Log*

Novels by Sharon Lee

The Carousel Trilogy: *Carousel Tides* * *Carousel Sun* * *Carousel Seas*

Jennifer Pierce Maine Mysteries: *Barnburner* * *Gunshy*

Pinbeam Books Publications

Sharon Lee and Steve Miller's indie publishing arm

Adventures in the Liaden Universe®: *Two Tales of Korval* * *Fellow Travelers* * *Duty Bound* * *Certain Symmetry* * *Trading in Futures* * *Changeling* * *Loose Cannon* * *Shadows and Shades* * *Quiet Knives* * *With Stars Underfoot* * *Necessary Evils* * *Allies* * *Dragon Tide* * *Eidolon* * *Misfits* * *Halfling Moon* **Skyblaze* * *Courier Run* * *Legacy Systems* * *Moon's Honor* * *Technical Details* * *Sleeping with the Enemy* * *Change Management* * *Due Diligence* * *Cultivar* * *Heirs to Trouble* * *Degrees of Separation* * *Fortune's Favor* * *Shout of Honor* * *The Gate that Locks the Tree* * *Ambient Conditions* * *Change State*

Splinter Universe Presents: *Splinter Universe Presents: Volume One* * *The Wrong Lance*

By Sharon Lee: *Variations Three* * *Endeavors of Will* * *The Day they Brought the Bears to Belfast* * *Surfside* * *The Gift of Magic* * *Spell Bound* * *Writing Neep*

By Steve Miller: *Chariot to the Stars* * *TimeRags II*

By Sharon Lee and Steve Miller: *Calamity's Child* * *The Cat's Job* * *Master Walk* * *Quiet Magic* * *The Naming of Kinzel* * *Reflections on Tinsori Light*

THANK YOU

Thank you for your support of our work.

Sharon Lee and Steve Miller